Acting Edition

Sancocho

by Christin Eve Cato

||SAMUEL FRENCH||

FOR PRODUCTION INQUIRIES

UNITED STATES AND CANADA
info@concordtheatricals.com
1-866-979-0447

UNITED KINGDOM AND EUROPE
licensing@concordtheatricals.co.uk
020-7054-7298

Each title is subject to availability from Concord Theatricals Corp., depending upon country of performance. Please be aware that *SANCOCHO* may not be licensed by Concord Theatricals Corp. in your territory. Professional and amateur producers should contact the nearest Concord Theatricals Corp. office or licensing partner to verify availability.

No one shall make any changes in this title(s) for the purpose of production. No part of this book may be reproduced, stored in a retrieval system, scanned, uploaded, or transmitted in any form, by any means, now known or yet to be invented, including mechanical, electronic, digital, photocopying, recording, videotaping, or otherwise, without the prior written permission of the publisher. No one shall share this title(s), or any part of this title(s), through any social media or file hosting websites.

For all inquiries regarding motion picture, television, online/digital and other media rights, please contact Concord Theatricals Corp.

MUSIC AND THIRD-PARTY MATERIALS USE NOTE

Licensees are solely responsible for obtaining formal written permission from copyright owners to use copyrighted music and/or other copyrighted third-party materials (e.g. artworks, logos) in the performance of this play and are strongly cautioned to do so. If no such permission is obtained by the licensee, then the licensee must use only original music and materials that the licensee owns and controls. Licensees are solely responsible and liable for clearances of all third-party copyrighted materials, including without limitation music, and shall indemnify the copyright owners of the play(s) and their licensing agent, Concord Theatricals Corp., against any costs, expenses, losses and liabilities arising from the use of such copyrighted third-party materials by licensees. For music, please contact the appropriate music licensing authority in your territory for the rights to any incidental music.

IMPORTANT BILLING AND CREDIT REQUIREMENTS

If you have obtained performance rights to this title, please refer to your licensing agreement for important billing and credit requirements.

The Off-Broadway premiere of *SANCOCHO* was produced by Latinx Playwrights Circle, WP Theater, and The Sol Project at the WP Theater in New York on March 11, 2023. The performance was directed by Rebecca Martínez, with scenic design by Raul Abrego, costume design by Harry Nadal, lighting design by María Cristina Fusté, and sound design by Germán Martínez. The cast was as follows:

CARIDAD DE JESÚS . . . . .Zuleyma Guevara
RENATA DE JESÚS-PEREZ . . . . .Shirley Rumierk

The midwest premiere of *SANCOCHO* was produced by Vision Latino Theatre Company, Chicago, IL, on October 10, 2022. The performance was directed by Xavier M. Custodio, with scenic design by Shayna Patel, costume design by Yajaira Custodio, lighting design by Sebastian "SeaBass" Medina, and technical direction by Line Bower. The cast was as follows:

CARIDAD DE JESÚS . . . . Antonia Arcely
RENATA DE JESÚS-PEREZ . . . . .Amber Lee Ramos

SANCOCHO was originally developed by the Latinx Playwrights Circle.

CHARACTERS

CARIDAD DE JESÚS – Fifty-eight years old, Puerto Rican, the matriarch of the family (Renata's sister). She has dark skin, inherited from her African ancestors. She's a keeper of tradition and ritual.

RENATA DE JESÚS-PEREZ – Thirty-three years old, Puerto Rican, a lawyer (Caridad's sister). She has light skin, inherited from her European ancestors. She is dedicated to searching for and upholding the truth.

SETTING

New York City, El Barrio. A pre-war apartment building.

A modest kitchen decorated with roosters, wooden spoons, ceramic plates that say "Puerto Rico" on them, and shelves full of spices. The fridge is covered with magnets and pictures of kids' birthdays, weddings, and school portraits, family get-togethers, coupons, receipts, and bill reminders. On top of the fridge is a portable radio. On top of the stove is a pot. The kitchen table sits in the center of the stage. On top of the table are various vegetables, a chef knife, and a cutting board. On the other side of the stage is a living room/area space with an altar set up. There are various picture frames and candles on top of it.

Somewhere in the room, perhaps on a shelf, is the book *One Hundred Years of Solitude* by Gabriel García Márquez.

TIME

Fall 2023.

AUTHOR'S NOTES

"/" means to overlap in the place where it starts

"–" means to cut off the other person's sentence

Caridad and Renata should actually be cooking in real time.

SANCOCHO FAMILY TIMELINE

Cidra, PR:
September 1965
Caridad De Jesús and Candido De Jesús (twins) are born to Mildred De Jesús, nineteen years old (Mami), and Hector De Jesús, twenty-four years old (Papi).

December 1965
Candido passes away from infancy complications.

El Barrio, East Harlem:
June 1966
Caridad, Mami, Papi, and Julia Marín (Abuela/Mami's mother) move to NYC.

March 1969
Eduardo (Eddie) García De Jesús is born, the offspring of Papi's extramarital affair.

April 1979
(1979 Recession and Energy Crisis in America) Papi loses the bodega; Mami's arthritis causes her to lose her factory job.

January 1980
Caridad drops out of high school to help with bills and care for her parents.

September 1981
Caridad gets her GED.

August 1983
Abuela passes away from heart conditions.

May 1986
Caridad meets Juan Rodriguez.

July 1986
Eddie unexpectedly visits the De Jesús residence and meets Papi; Caridad and Mami suffer physical trauma inflicted by Papi; Caridad leaves Mami and Papi's house and gets engaged to Juan.

September 1987
Caridad and Juan get married.

September 1989
Papi has a stroke.

July 1990
Renata De Jesús is born to Mildred and Hector De Jesús.

January 1991

Caridad gives birth to Sergio and Lydia Rodriguez.

November 2002

Caridad leaves Juan and kicks him out of their lives.

June 2008

Renata graduates from high school.

August 2008

Renata starts college and stays close to home. Renata meets Carlos Perez.

June 2009

Sergio and Lydia graduate from high school.

December 2010

Mami's cousins from Puerto Rico visit. Sergio meets his girlfriend and moves in with her. Renata and Carlos begin dating.

May 2012

Renata graduates from college. Lydia gets married. Mami starts showing signs of dementia.

May 2015

Renata graduates from Fordham Law School.

September 2015

Mami gets placed into hospice care.

October 2015

Renata and Carlos get married.

November 2016

Mami passes away from Alzheimer's.

February 2019

Caridad is reunited with Eddie at Sergio's car wash.

WORDS TO KNOW

Shortened and slang words are used throughout the script to reflect Puerto Rican/Nuyorican vernacular.

Ajo – Garlic

Ay – pronounced like "I"; is an expression often used for sighing, (Ex. "Ugh," "Oh my," "Oy vey")

Bemba – big lips (slang)

Bendito – to be blessed; a term used for expressing empathy and often pity; it is also often used sarcastically

Bolitas – mini balls

Boricua – the Indigenous Taíno word for a person born in the island of Borikén (original name of Puerto Rico)

Borrachos – drunk people

Carajo – an expression/interjection that denotes anger and/or frustration; it is also commonly used to tell someone to go to hell – "vete pal carajo" (go to hell)

Carajo – fuck (slang)

Cáscara – skin; peel

Cualquiera – any (feminine); any woman/any strange woman

Cubito – little cube (slang)

Desgraciá – shortened version of desgraciada; ungrateful/miserable girl!

Estúpida – stupid (feminine); this term is widely used to offend someone or to playfully undermine someone

Finca – farm

Gracias – thank you

Iglesia – church

Jíbaro/Jíbara – hick (masculine/feminine); hillbilly; country person

Las noticias – the news

Limpieza – a cleanse; a spiritual/energetic cleansing

Locura – craziness

Malcriá – shortened version of malcriada; a spoiled brat (feminine)

Mija – my daughter; often arbitrarily used by elders as an endearing way to address a younger person they are close to

Mijo – my son; often arbitrarily used by elders as an endearing way to address a younger person they are close to

Mira – look

Misa – church mass

Negrita – a Black girl; often used endearingly towards a loved one who is of darker skin, or condescendingly towards a person of darker skin

Nena – an endearing pronoun for a girl/young woman

Pelitos – little hairs

Pendeja – asshole (feminine); stupid girl; this term is widely used to offend someone or to playfully undermine someone

Pilón – an Indigenous/traditional Puerto Rican mortar and pestle

Plátano – plantain fruit

Porquería – bullshit; filth

Puñeta – damn; damnit (slang)

Rabitos – oxtails

Sala – living room

Sancocho – a traditional Puerto Rican stew made with oxtail and root vegetables

Sofrito – a Latino-Caribbean seasoning made from fresh vegetables and ingredients

Sucia – dirty (feminine); a woman who is dirty-minded

Timbre – doorbell; buzzer

Verdad – truth; right

Viejo – old man

Ya – an expression for "enough," "that's it," "already"

Sancocho Familia Tree

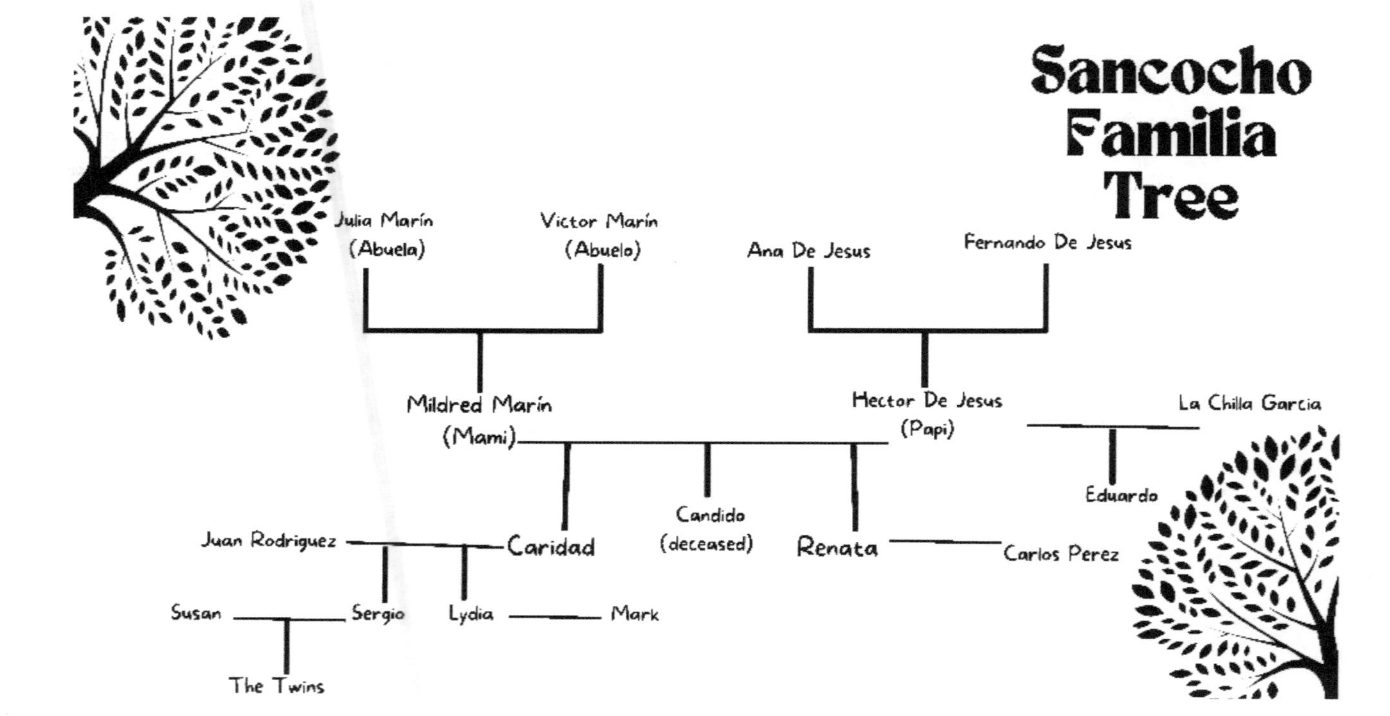

Para mi abuelita, Julia:
Mi inspiración, mi musa, La diosa que me enseñó a cocinar sancocho.

[For my grandmother, Julia:
My inspiration, my muse, the goddess who taught me how to cook
sancocho.]

"Verily, verily, I say unto you,
except a corn of wheat fall into the ground and die, it abideth alone:
but if it die, it bringeth forth much fruit"

– John 12:24 (The King James Holy Bible)

<h1 style="text-align:center">Scene One</h1>

<h2 style="text-align:center">In The Beginning</h2>

(AT RISE: The aroma of a lived-in kitchen, something is always cooking on the stove. **CARIDAD**, *buzzing around in her apron, tidying up the kitchen. She pours herself a glass of red wine. The sound of cardinals singing is heard as she pours the wine. She pauses to notice the bird's song. She eventually sits at the table and starts peeling carrots. Then after a few moments, we hear a toilet flush.* **RENATA** *enters, wobbling, holding her pregnant belly. She joins* **CARIDAD**. **CARIDAD** *continues chopping.)*

RENATA. I have to get back to Jersey before the traffic is insane.

CARIDAD. Traffic is always insane in El Barrio. Carlos called while you were in the bathroom.

*(***RENATA*** grunts.)*

RENATA. *(Muttering to herself.)* Ugh what does he want now?

(She grabs her phone and checks it, texting Carlos.)

CARIDAD. I don't know, maybe he's checking on his *pregnant wife?* What's the problem?

RENATA. You really wanna get me started?

*(***CARIDAD*** silently insists.)*

RENATA. Everything, honestly. It's like – his mannerisms. You know? He gets on my nerves sometimes.

CARIDAD. Who, Carlos? *No me diga.*[1] What the hell did he do?

RENATA. I just don't like the way he moves around…he's clumsy, he washes dishes with one hand and leaves the lip stains on the glasses, he pokes at his phone screen so hard when he's typing on it that sometimes I feel like he's gonna break it! He never finishes a cup of coffee, and he always leaves one spoonful of rice on the plate. Like it's just one more spoon, just fucking eat it.

CARIDAD. Wow…

RENATA. Ugh, and he has this diddy bop! I mean I guess I never really noticed it before, but I definitely notice it now! Sometimes I hate walking behind him on the street.

CARIDAD. I think you're just being hormonal. *Bendito, pobre Carlos.*

RENATA. But then he also has this bad habit of going to bed wearing the same socks he had on all day. Isn't that unsanitary and freaking disgusting?

CARIDAD. Ay fo,[2] sí. That's nasty.

RENATA. Right?! And so I yell at him about it, I'm like, "Come on Carlos, do you have to be so fucking nasty? Take off those dingy stinky socks that you've had on all day!" And then he's like, "Shut up, Renata, they're not dirty, they're clean, I just put them on today!"

CARIDAD. Ay, is he really that childish?

(**RENATA** *nods furiously.*)

RENATA. So, whatever, we always have this rendezvous where I get all pissed off and I give him an ultimatum: either take off those damn socks or sleep on the sofa!

---

1. Oh, you don't say.
2. Eww!

CARIDAD. You really have to try to control your mood swings.

> (**CARIDAD** *starts chopping the carrots. A slight pause from* **RENATA**.)

RENATA. Really, Cari? *Mood swings?* You should be the last one / to talk about *moods*.

CARIDAD. / Carlos worships the ground you walk on. The way he looks at you with those big loving eyes. He does everything for you.

RENATA. I know, I know, I know… I just hope my daughter doesn't come out with that *diddy bop*.

CARIDAD. ¿Pero qué carajo es un diddy bop?[3] He walks like any average person. Don't be so mean.

RENATA. Anyway, did you take a look at those documents?

> (**CARIDAD** *continues chopping, a little annoyed that* **RENATA** *is changing the subject.*)

CARIDAD. So, dime.[4] What are you eating these days? Your skin looks good.

RENATA. Why are you changing the subject?

CARIDAD. You changed it first.

(She continues chopping.)

RENATA. I eat the usual stuff that my doctor recommends. Lots of avocados. Healthy fats.

Fish for Omega-3s. Brown rice for carbs. Berries for the extra hydration and antioxidants. I take my vitamins.

CARIDAD. Has your doctor told you anything else?

RENATA. That I might have to get induced. I thought I told you.

---

3. But what the hell is a diddy bop?
4. Tell me.

CARIDAD. No I don't remember you telling me that.

RENATA. Well it made me really sad because I wanted to give birth in the pool.

CARIDAD. *Right.* Yes. I do remember you telling me *that...*

RENATA. What?

CARIDAD. Nothing.

RENATA. Why do you have that judgy face on?

CARIDAD. What judgy face?

RENATA. Just spit it out.

CARIDAD. No, nada... Es que,[1] you young girls are always jumping on the newest trend.

RENATA. It's not a *trend.* Water births have been a thing since forever –

CARIDAD. I was in labor for twelve hours with my twins, had them naturally too. I didn't need a *pool...*

Pero, the water must be soothing for the baby. ¿Qué se yo?[2]

RENATA. Of course it is... I mean just imagine it, a baby, who from since conception, is immersed in the warmth of its mother's womb. Comforted by the soothing amniotic fluid that supports breathing, growth, and nutrients. Imagine being used to all of that and then suddenly you're pushed out headfirst! Into this strange atmosphere called "air."

CARIDAD. Bendito, and then someone slaps your ass just to make sure you're alive.

RENATA. Then they swaddle you up in sterilized, synthetic cotton –

---

1. No, nothing...it's that,
2. What do I know?

CARIDAD. And the first person to hold you is not even tu mamá. It's some cualquiera.

RENATA. Yeah! And then finally after a pass around or two, they hand you off to your mother who has been longing to hold you from the moment you were just a possibility.

CARIDAD. Well, you could only hope that she's had that longing. Not every mother chooses to be a mother –

RENATA. So you somehow just wish that you will be contaminated with joy in an antiseptic room.

CARIDAD. Mmmhmm. That's why Mami had us naturally. No epidural. No hospitals. Abuela era una doula también, sabes?[3] Pero *you??* No – you were born in a hospital because you nearly killed Mami –

RENATA. Did you really have to go there? We were doing so well, Cari.

(**CARIDAD** *sips her wine.*)

CARIDAD. Mira, it's just that, I think about what women have endured for ages, you know? Y aquí estamos[4] in a new age, you're healthy, seven months pregnant – and you have this *doctor* not even giving you the chance to have this baby on your own. Telling you to induce it with chemicals? ¿Qué clase de mierda es esa?[5]

RENATA. Caridad, these procedures are standard now. Medicine has evolved.

CARIDAD. Your body has been equipped to give birth!! Sometimes we aren't even aware of what we are made of until we are forced to meet with God, face to face.

(**RENATA** *looks at the glass of red wine.*)

---

3. Abuela was a birth doula too, you know?
4. And here we are
5. What type of shit is that?

RENATA. How many of those have you had already?

CARIDAD. You know I like to sip on the blood of Christ as I am preparing the food that sustains everlasting life. It's ritual.

RENATA. Yeah, well take it easy. This ain't the last supper.

CARIDAD. Can you grab the pilón and smash some garlic? You love to eat but you never want to help.

RENATA. Caridad. You know I didn't come here to eat and hang out. Did you take a look at those documents? It's important. / It's Papi's will.

CARIDAD. / You telling me you not gonna eat my food?

RENATA. But sancocho takes forever to make. What's the occasion anyway?

CARIDAD. It's Sunday.

RENATA. And? What is it, you're hosting Sunday dinners now?

CARIDAD. Yes, I think it will be a nice tradition to start. So, if you want to talk about those documents, I suggest you rest your feet for a little while longer.

RENATA. I have work to do, papers to prepare. I have a job, you know? Tomorrow is the start of the new work week –

CARIDAD. Yeah, yeah – I know how *important* you are.

> (**CARIDAD** *grabs the pilón and places it on the table while* **RENATA** *reluctantly returns to her seat and starts peeling garlic.* **CARIDAD** *returns with house slippers for* **RENATA**.)

RENATA. You're lucky I'm eating for two.

CARIDAD. Lucky? I shoulda played the lotto then.

(**RENATA** *puts on the slippers. They're silent for a little while and it's awkward.* **RENATA** *begins to smash the garlic and a piece of garlic flies out of the pilón.*)

You gotta add salt to it.

RENATA. Why?

CARIDAD. It keeps it inside the pilón.

RENATA. Ahhh, the little tricks...

CARIDAD. Abuela taught me that.

RENATA. I wish I could've met her.

(*A beat.*)

I wish a lot of things.

CARIDAD. Like what? Please don't mention / Carlos.

RENATA. I'm not talking about / Carlos.

CARIDAD. Then what? What more could you possibly wish for?

RENATA. I wish Mami taught me how to cook.

CARIDAD. You're learning how to cook right now. Stop with the whining already, carajo –

RENATA. I'm just expressing my thoughts. Gosh, Cari –

CARIDAD. Okay, okay...express your *thoughts*.

RENATA. I was thinking about this the other day actually – like *why* didn't she teach me how to cook? Why did she forbid me from the kitchen? That wasn't fair. We could've bonded more, you know?

CARIDAD. Forbid you? She didn't *forbid* you. No sea' pendeja –

RENATA. I'm not a / pendeja –

CARIDAD. / She wanted you to focus on your studies. Okay? You came out intelligent, speaking full sentences by the time you were two. She didn't want to bother you with chores, she wanted you to be a career woman. You should consider yourself lucky. Not many girls get that luxury. She raised you up like the way we raise up boys: "Don't worry about cooking and washing clothes mijo, all you have to worry about is getting a good job and being a good provider."

RENATA. Oh, you mean like how you raised up Sergio to be?

    (**CARIDAD** *gives her a look – something like "don't be talking about Sergio" and starts chopping the potatoes.)*

CARIDAD. You don't realize what she did for you, eh? You never had to worry about the burdens that women are inherited with. She let you be yourself, to grow up curious about the world. She didn't make you clean, she made you read books. When you came home from school, you came home to a bed that was made, ropa limpia, y comida hecha.[1] Even with Papi you were lucky. He was easy on you. Don't be such a malcriá,[2] it's offensive.

RENATA. I never said I wasn't grateful for those things! But I'm not kidding when I say she used to literally throw me out of the kitchen if I was in there while she was cooking. And then when her arthritis got worse, she cooked less. And when the dementia took over – that was it! I missed that window, you know?

CARIDAD. Did it ever occur to you that Papi was the one who told Mami to not bother you with learning how to do domestic things? That you were *too good* for it and that you had better things to be learning?

---

1. clean clothes and cooked food
2. spoiled brat

RENATA. That makes no sense. Why would Papi even say that? Everyone should know how to make food, it's survival.

(**CARIDAD** *starts laughing.*)

CARIDAD. For someone who's so smart, you're so naive.

RENATA. And you're cynical and dysfunctional.

CARIDAD. Mira, ten cuidao conmigo, okay?[3]

(*She continues chopping the potatoes.*)

RENATA. This is serious for me. I'm about to be a mother now and I want to be like how you and Mami were. I want my child to come home from school and have homemade lunch.

Papitas con huevo frito[4] made with love. I want to be the mom that cooks a wholesome dinner every night. My child deserves that too. *I'm* supposed to pass that down to *her.*

CARIDAD. Ay Renata, cooking is easy. If you want to learn, then you'll learn. It's not rocket science. You're a lawyer, for Christ's sake. Act like you have a brain, nena.

RENATA. And while you're at it, act like you're grateful and don't forget how my *lawyer* money is taking care of Papi's hospice bills, okay?

CARIDAD. Just don't be an exagerá'. That's all I'm saying.

RENATA. I'm not exaggerating! How could anyone expect me to learn how to cook when I had all these things I had to do, huh? After an eight-hour day of school, I either had choir practice or karate lessons or softball practice or math tutoring! And yeah, by the time I came home dinner was already cooked! And then I had tons of homework to do. And forget about it, once college happened –

---

3. Hey, be careful with me, okay?
4. French fries with fried eggs

CARIDAD. You were the first to go to college / you're welcome!

RENATA. / I was always studying. And then by the time I went to law school, I had no house skills. I had to drop off my laundry because I sucked at washing clothes. I lived on pizza, frozen dinners, and Chinese takeout!

CARIDAD. *Ay bendito, la pobrecita.*[1] And now you're making all this *lawyer money* – you can hire your own chef!

RENATA. No! It's not the same, Caridad! IT'S NOT THE FUCKING SAME!

>   (**CARIDAD** *finishes her glass of wine and refills another.*)

CARIDAD. No te puedo creer.[2] You have exactly what you need and you still complain. You can't be everything.

RENATA. Well what else am I supposed to be? My kid's not gonna have a Puerto Rican grandmother – who's gonna pass down those cultural roots to her? I mean she will have Carlos's parents. And I *love* that, you know? I think Mexican culture is beautiful, I really do. I just... my kid should feel Puerto Rican too.

CARIDAD. Then when she gets older, send her to Puerto Rico for the summer. They have those immersive programs. It would make her fluent en español tambien.

RENATA. That's not what I mean though. She needs to grow up eating Puerto Rican food. Food is the direct connection to our roots. It tells us the history of our people, way before language gets involved into the mix –

CARIDAD. Don't tell me you're talking about how Spanish is bad now. That's our language, it's what we speak,

---

1. The poor girl.
2. I can't believe you.

okay? What's that thing that kids are talking about nowadays? Este, *recolonization*?

RENATA. It's *decolonization*. But yes, decolonizing our food is good too. Getting rid of shit like vienna sausages –

CARIDAD. Then how we gonna make *arroz con salchichas*?

RENATA. I don't know – by using actual *pork*?!

CARIDAD. *Ay ya!* We are always wishing for the things we don't have Renata. The grass is always greener across the street. Si no es esto, es lo otro.[3]

RENATA. Oh trust me, I KNOW how insatiable we are as human beings. It's in our nature to never be satisfied.

CARIDAD. Maybe for someone like you.

RENATA. I don't really want one of your red wine lectures, Cari.

CARIDAD. I'm not drunk, pendeja. Relax.

RENATA. Not yet.

> (**CARIDAD** *shoots* **RENATA** *a look and takes a sip of her wine.*)

All I meant was that I wish I knew how to cook. Yes I can learn now, but I wanted to learn *her* ways. The way she made sofrito from scratch, the dough for the pastelillos, arroz con guandules without it coming out clunky, the way she made pernil perfectly succulent, and the way she made oxtail slide off the bone –

CARIDAD. Mofongo that wasn't too dry, bacalao that wasn't too salty –

RENATA. Yes! And the way she made sancocho that was healing after a long and stressful week...

CARIDAD. I use her same recipe. The same one Abuela taught her. So aprende, nena. Learn.

---

3. If it's not one thing, it's another.

(**RENATA** *continues to smash the garlic. But then she starts smashing harder, and harder, and harder.*)

CARIDAD. Jesucristo, what did the ajo ever do to you?

(**RENATA** *keeps smashing.*)

¿Qué te pasa?[1]

RENATA. We have to talk about Papi. What are we gonna do –

CARIDAD. He's dying, what else is there to do for him?

RENATA. Cari, we have to go over logistics. Papi can die any day now, we should be planning his funeral, his memorial service, his –

CARIDAD. All your generation cares about is getting down to business. Going online. Texting on your phones. You forget about quality time. When's the last time I saw you, huh?

(**RENATA** *laughs.*)

RENATA. *Quality time?* When was the last time seeing each other had any quality?

CARIDAD. All these quick visits and five-minute phone calls. That's not how family works!

RENATA. All you do is criticize me left and right! Is that how family works?

CARIDAD. *Lo hago de cariño.*[2] Tough love.

RENATA. Tough love is throwing a kid into a pool to see if they swim. Putting a child on a bike and letting go –

CARIDAD. That sounds like premeditated murder to me.

(**RENATA** *looks at the smashed garlic in the pilón.*)

---

1. What's bothering you?
2. I do it out of care.

RENATA. So, what's next?

CARIDAD. Ahhh, so you like this, huh?

RENATA. You're literally holding me hostage right now.

CARIDAD. The onions are next.

> (**CARIDAD** *takes an onion and peels off the skin with a knife. She takes the skin and puts it inside of a Ziploc bag that she removes from the freezer.*)

RENATA. You're saving the onion peels?

CARIDAD. To make more broth later.

RENATA. Really? Scraps, though?

CARIDAD. You know what's disgusting? *Swanson broth.* It's better to save all of your vegetable scraps. Especially any tomatoes, garlic, onions, carrots, celery, recao –

RENATA. Re-qué?

CARIDAD. *Ay bendito.* Are you really this clueless? *Recao.* It's our version of cilantro. We use it to make the sofrito. Pero, you don't want to put too much of it when you make the broth. It will come out bitter. You can also add parsley –

RENATA. Oh I love parsley!

CARIDAD. Yeah... I know.

RENATA. What's that supposed to mean?

CARIDAD. Nada, es que I know you just love making your gringo pasta with store-bought meat sauce, topped with the dried parsley that comes in a shaker, sided with frozen garlic bread you pop into the oven. Mmhmm. I know.

RENATA. Wow, Caridad... so you telling me I won't find a box of Barilla pasta / in your cabinet right now?!

CARIDAD. Qué? It's not true? You don't make boxed mashed potatoes either?

RENATA. No, it's not true. I boil my own potatoes, smash them and then add butter.

> (**CARIDAD** *gives her a disgusted look – those mashed potatoes sound like they need help!*)

CARIDAD. Bland –

RENATA. And I actually buy fresh parsley that I chop myself AND I also buy parmesan cheese by the block that I shave myself! I also skip on the bread. Too much carbs.

CARIDAD. So anyway, once you have enough scraps you boil it in some water, add salt, pepper, and achiote, and let it simmer for about twenty-five to thirty minutes.

> (**RENATA** *takes out her phone.*)

RENATA. How do you spell achoota?

CARIDAD. A-CH-I-OTE. There's an "i" in it. You don't have to google it nena, it's right there on the shelf. Those little red seeds...they have a nice smokey flavor and they are a natural food coloring. Taínos used this too, you know?

RENATA. *(Looking at her phone.)* Hmmm, achiote is also known as the lipstick tree. Cute!

CARIDAD. *Tú y tu Google.*[1]

RENATA. Tú y tu judgments...

> (**CARIDAD** *starts to chop the onions.*)

CARIDAD. You got something against judges, *Ms. Abogada*?[2] I'm a Virgo, we make the best judges, it's in my nature. *You*, on the other hand...a Cancer? Too emotional.

---

1. You and your Google.
2. Ms. Lawyer

RENATA. Yeah I could never understand your *hypocrisy,* how you can be so Catholic and still worship Walter Mercado –

CARIDAD. Qué Dios lo bendiga![3]

RENATA. Sorry! May Walter Mercado rest in his power.

CARIDAD. Con mucho, mucho –

> *(They each kiss their fingers [a la Walter Mercado] and blow the kiss to the air.)*

CARIDAD & RENATA. Amor!

CARIDAD. Abuela y Mami never missed a Walter Mercado reading.

RENATA. Mami would hush up the entire house whenever his segment came on.

CARIDAD. Abuela used to do the same.

RENATA. What was Abuela's zodiac sign?

CARIDAD. *Sagitario.*

RENATA. Oh that's fun.

CARIDAD. Yes, she was a trip. She was a God-fearing woman who loved to tell inappropriate jokes.

RENATA. Tell me one.

CARIDAD. Cuando me levanto por la mañana, lo primero que hago es meterlo dentro. ¿Qué es?[4]

> **(RENATA** *picks up on the sexual innuendo.)*

RENATA. Put *what* inside?

CARIDAD. Mis pies en chancletas.[5]

> **(RENATA** *kind of giggles.)*

---

3. May God bless him!
4. When I wake up in the morning, the first thing I do is put it inside. What is it?
5. My feet in slippers.

RENATA. That's corny.

CARIDAD. I'm not the comedian of the family. Abuela had
better timing. It's all about delivery, right *abogada*?

> (*They continue chopping.* **RENATA** *picks up a
> yuca root and examines it.*)

That's yuca.

RENATA. I know what yuca is. It's just so...*ugly* looking.

CARIDAD. It's a root. This is how it looks before you peel
it naked.

> (**RENATA** *takes that as a [sexual] inside joke.*)

> (**CARIDAD** *may or may not say this, but she
> thinks it for sure:*)

> (*Sucia.*)

> (**RENATA** *gets on her phone.*)

RENATA. Like – who was the first person that was curious
enough to eat this? You know what I mean? Don't you
ever wonder about those things?

CARIDAD. Probably a Taíno. Yuca was precious to them.

RENATA. Actually – cassava originally comes from Brazil.
Just *googled* it.

CARIDAD. You believe anything they put on that damn
internet, don't you? Why don't you look up Yúcahu –

RENATA. Yuca-who?

CARIDAD. The *Taíno God of Yuca.*

> (**RENATA** *looks it up,* **CARIDAD** *is right.*)

RENATA. Since when have you been an expert on
Indigenous history?

CARIDAD. It's called *oral history*, nena. And you think you the only who reads in this family? I used to love the library back in the day... ay, those were some good times.

>   (**CARIDAD** *smiles and continues chopping the onions.*)

RENATA. Cari, are you crying?

CARIDAD. It's the onions *pendeja* –

RENATA. Stop calling me a pendeja, okay. I don't like it.

CARIDAD. Don't be so emotional –

RENATA. Stop fucking deflecting.

CARIDAD. Excuse me?

RENATA. You know what you're doing! Undermining me. I'm not a child anymore. I'm a grown ass woman –

CARIDAD. Yeah well you're acting like a spoiled little brat right now –

RENATA. This was a mistake! I thought that we could finally get together and have a decent fucking conversation. Because maybe, just maybe, you would understand that WE are all we have left in this family! / But no! That'll never happen. You won't let it!

CARIDAD. / Why do you think I called you over here, eh? For your stupid papers? *Cálmate, nena.*[1] Your hormones / are getting out of control.

RENATA.   HORMONES?! NO!! It's YOU Cari! YOU provoke me.

>   (*Renata's phone rings.*)

It's for work. I need to take this.

---

1. Calm down, girl.

*(She exits to take her call. **CARIDAD** continues chopping. The sound of birds is heard again. She looks around and sighs.)*

Scene Two

Head in the Sky

(A moment later. **CARIDAD** *is slicing some peppers.* **RENATA** *enters still on the phone. She is finishing up her call. She is sounding extra "professional." A stark difference from how she's been talking with Cari.)*

RENATA. *(On the phone.)* Thank you, so the seventh at eleven a.m.? Sounds great. Perfect. Have a great rest of your weekend. Buh-bye.

CARIDAD. *(Mocking* **RENATA***.) Buh-bye.*

*(***RENATA** *is visibly annoyed.)*

RENATA. This is why I talk to my therapist about you.

CARIDAD. You see a therapist?

RENATA. Yeah Cari, and you should too.

CARIDAD. That's what I have prayer for.

(She points to her altar.)

RENATA. It's clearly not enough.

CARIDAD. So what have you been talking about with this therapist of yours?

RENATA. That's none of your business.

CARIDAD. Well you obviously want to share something with me. Otherwise you wouldn't have mentioned it –

RENATA. Everything. Work, stress, childhood stuff –

CARIDAD. You really complain about your childhood? *¡Desgraciá!*[1]

---

1. Ungrateful/Miserable girl!

RENATA. Do you even remember my childhood? Like were you there? Because you out of ALL people should know that it wasn't all laughter and smiles!

CARIDAD. Oh, I was there alright! And you had everything you needed –

RENATA. Really? You just plan on sweeping this under the rug for the rest of your life? Not *everything* was fucking dealt with, Cari –

> (**CARIDAD** *starts to chop the pepper slices into cubes.*)

CARIDAD. Rena, you must be really out of your mind, huh?

RENATA. Stop gaslighting me –

CARIDAD. *Lighting gas?*

RENATA. Making me feel like there's something wrong with me when I'm perfectly in the right!

CARIDAD. Nobody is doing that nena!

RENATA. You're doing it right now! You and Mami both! No matter how well I was doing, you always had something to say. "Oh, she's so smart, she's in college... pero no, she can't even boil an egg or wash her own panties" –

CARIDAD. This is what you go to therapy for?

RENATA. But then you guys loved to boast about me to your friends like – "oh, Renata is doing so good, she's in law school, top in her class" ...You both even embellished sometimes, exaggerating... "Yeah and she got all the scholarships." HA! Scholarships my ass, I'm still paying off those motherfucking loans.

CARIDAD. I honestly thought you had tougher skin, girlfriend.

RENATA. The picking on me is what hurt the most. I remember this one time…it was that summer Mami's cousins came to visit us from Puerto Rico. We were all sitting in the sala,[1] relaxing. And it had been a great day. Like I took the cousins sightseeing and we went out shopping. I introduced them to babaganoush for the first time and they were in LOVE –

CARIDAD. Who the hell is *babaganú?*

RENATA. It's roasted eggplant. So, yeah – anyway, we took pictures by the pier and watched the sun set. Then we arrived to the house and Mami had been home all day I guess, because Papi was sick remember?

CARIDAD. *Dios mío*, when wasn't that man sick?

RENATA. And you could tell Mami had already been drinking before we got there. It wasn't bad or anything, but she was in one of those extra moods – you know, when everything is extra: her voice, her tone, her enthusiasm, her laugh…

(**RENATA** *remembers her mother's laugh.*)

CARIDAD. And? Can you get to the freaking point / already? *Carajo.*

(**CARIDAD** *finishes her glass of wine.*)

RENATA. So, there we all were, in the sala reunited again. They were speaking highly of me, and I just felt validated. And you know I'm not an egotistical person –

CARIDAD. *(Sarcastically.)* Who you? Oh, never –

RENATA. Seriously though. I've always stayed to myself, a loner who spent her time with a book in her face. And I guess I loved their praise because I thought the world of them. They were sweet and spiritual. The good kind of spiritual.

---

1. living room

CARIDAD. That's true. I'll give you that. Really good people.

RENATA. But forget it. That high got buzz-killed when Mami started criticizing me. I can't remember exactly what she said, but it was something about me always needing money and that I was too lazy to get a job, or some insulting shit like that. It was so mean and condescending. And I thought at that moment – "Mami, why would you put me down like that? I'm your daughter." You know? Like fuck, I was still in college –

CARIDAD. Pero era la verdad.[1] Mami and Papi were scraping for money during that time. You thinking you were too good to work because you were in school –

RENATA. Oh my God!!! See what I mean?! No! No, that was not the case. I was doing everything they expected me to do. I was working that summer. I had an internship. A full-time one. An unpaid one. And I fucking worked hard at that internship. She didn't get it. Working another part-time summer job to make a quick buck was the last thing on my mind. It's not how the game works. You gotta play hard to win hard.

CARIDAD. You know, it's possible that she maybe resented you –

RENATA. What the fuck are you suggesting?

CARIDAD. I know you hate to hear it, but Mami wasn't planning on having you. She was old, *puñeta*. Damn near forty-four.

RENATA. That's not *old*.

CARIDAD. For someone who was in her condition? With diabetes and high blood pressure? Yes it was. You weren't supposed to be conceived, but it happened –

RENATA. And why would Mami resent me for that? I didn't ask to be born.

---

1. But it was the truth.

CARIDAD. It's the *how* she got pregnant –

RENATA. No! I'm NOT gonna go down this rabbit hole with you! Whatever happened wasn't my fucking fault! …You know what? You get verbally abusive just like her when you drink. That's why you should stop! You're a drunk just like Mami, just like Papi –

CARIDAD. Excuse me! Don't you ever compare me to Papi!

(**RENATA** *stands up.*)

You leaving?

RENATA. Yeah Cari, you're triggering me now –

CARIDAD. Pero we still need the plátanos, corn, and the rabitos are in the fridge marinating in sofrito – Ay! I gotta put them to simmer now. / They take so long to get tender and you want them to slide right off the bone.

RENATA. / I'm done with this conversation.

CARIDAD. You can't leave yet! We're not done talking, Rena.

RENATA. But you're the one who doesn't wanna talk about anything I want to talk about!

CARIDAD. Okay, okay! *Habla.*

RENATA. I want to discuss Papi's will with you because there are certain details that you need to know. Why haven't you looked at the document?

CARIDAD. Because you're the lawyer here! What do you need my input for? Why do you even think I care what's in his damned will?

RENATA. First of all, you're his eldest daughter.

CARIDAD. And he made you his proxy, so go ahead. I could care less. *Qué will, y qué will…* All that he left me behind are bad memories –

RENATA. Cari, can we please have a real and honest conversation here? Like adults? Like civilized / people?

CARIDAD. Oh so now I'm not civilized! *¡No me faltes el respeto!*[1]

RENATA. You think it's *me* who lacks respect?! Look at how you talk about your dying father! Un-fucking-believable.

CARIDAD. You come to *my* house talking about *my* drinking / how *I'm* verbally abusive!

RENATA. / You're gonna make my blood pressure go up, Jesús Christ!

CARIDAD. ¡Relájate, nena! ...

> (*A moment.* **CARIDAD** *puts the oxtail in the pot, gently adding broth as she tosses the meat around. She also adds the smashed garlic and chopped onions.*)

Ginger is good for high blood pressure.

> (**RENATA** *watches and breathes in deeply to reduce stress. There is a musicality to the way that* **CARIDAD** *moves.*)

It's swift. It's almost magical. The aroma is everything. The sound of the sizzles is relaxing.

RENATA. That smells good.

CARIDAD. Meat, garlic, onions, peppers and broth. Always so good.

> (**CARIDAD** *keeps stirring.* **RENATA** *thinks for a moment.*)

RENATA. This is all just very taxing on my emotions. That Mami isn't here. I always imagined her being around

---

1. You lack respect!

to see my first baby. I'm still grieving from her passing, you know? It was a brutal one.

CARIDAD. It was really painful to see her go out like that. *Bendito. Un mundo desconocido.*[2] It still hurts me too. It's been seven years and the wound is still open.

RENATA. And now Papi is dying because of his failing kidneys. And like, here I am pregnant, reviewing his will and eventually writing his eulogy. I'm scared I'm gonna birth a sad child. That trauma is real, Cari. It gets passed down.

CARIDAD. What are you talking about? What gets passed down?

RENATA. Your kids can inherit your trauma. I'm talking about the trauma we pass down to our children while they are growing inside of us –

CARIDAD. Nena, I've had plenty of trauma in my day and I'm telling you it's going to be fine. Just make sure you show your baby love and attention. That's all a kid needs, Renata. Love and attention. Don't worry about passing down a trauma. I doubt that's even true.

RENATA. It's scientifically proven. There have been studies. Biological alterations in the DNA.

CARIDAD. These are all theories, Renata. I mean come on, nena...that's not science. That's just people thinking. What's that called again? A hypathosis?

RENATA. *Hypothesis –*

CARIDAD. Algo así, qué se yo –[3]

RENATA. I'm talking about generational trauma, Cari. The possibility that we can genetically pass on our PTSD to our children.

---

2. A world unknown.
3. Something like that, I don't know.

CARIDAD. *(Matter-of-factly.)* My kids are fine! Sergio has a car wash that he owns. He makes good money. His wife is wonderful and they have two beautiful boys. And Lydia is doing good too. She's not too smart, but she married good. Hopefully she'll have a baby soon too.

   (Beat.)

RENATA. What about their dad?

CARIDAD. What about him? Why are you even mentioning him?

RENATA. You don't think they felt any loss? Lydia and Sergio adored their dad and they had no reason as to why he left. No idea that he was a fucking horrible human being. Must've been devastating for them, don't you think?

CARIDAD. They didn't need him! They had ME. I had to be a mother and a father to my kids. And I did it without anyone's help! I spent hours on my knees cleaning floors and scrubbing toilets! I could've taken him to court for child support, but fuck that! I didn't need him and I was gonna prove it!

RENATA. You're really going to act like that, huh? Like it was *his* choice to leave?

CARIDAD. ¿De qué estás hablando?[1]

   (She crosses over to the stove to add more broth to the meat.)

RENATA. Your ex-husband. Juan. He didn't really leave, did he?

CARIDAD. Don't you dare, Renata!

RENATA. You're in so much denial that it's sad. You always said he left you, but I know you threw him out. I know you kicked him out. And Sergio and Lydia don't even know the truth about their own father do they?!

---

1. What are you talking about?

CARIDAD. Renata, I'm warning you!

RENATA. That he's a fucking molester! A pedophile!

CARIDAD. *¡Cállate!*

> (**CARIDAD** *takes the wooden spoon and raises it over* **RENATA***'s head.*)

RENATA. You're gonna hit me, Cari?! Is that your answer? Violence?! Drinking, verbal abuse and violence?!

> (**CARIDAD** *lowers the spoon and drops it into the sink. She's distraught. Hurt. She's not sure how to feel.*)

This is deeper than you, deeper than me! *We* could have inherited trauma ourselves. It's obvious, isn't it? Look at us. Look at YOU. This generational thing is true, Cari.

CARIDAD. Our people have also been healers, curanderos, and survivors...and that gets passed down too mija.

> (**RENATA** *is quiet. Rubbing her belly.* **CARIDAD** *drinks.*)

RENATA. I know. But talking about these things is the only way to get to the bottom of anything.

> (**CARIDAD** *feels the weight that* **RENATA** *feels.*)

CARIDAD. I couldn't look at him anymore. I hated him. I hated him for what he did to you. He didn't think I knew, but I fucking knew. You never told me, but you didn't have to.

RENATA. So it's true, you did really know.

> (**CARIDAD** *regrettably nods.*)

CARIDAD. I could see it in the look of his eyes. That nasty look. I regretted it every day... I hope that cabrón is dead.

RENATA. You know – this is the first time I've ever been able to talk about this with anyone in our family. We never spoke about these things. It was taboo, it was –

CARIDAD. I'm so sorry.

> (*A beat.* **CARIDAD** *wants to hug* **RENATA** *and* **RENATA** *wants to be hugged. They just can't bring themselves to do it just yet.*)

I couldn't look at you for a long time. I was angry. Maybe there was some envy there. You were a beautiful girl and everyone adored you. And... I don't know. I never ever got that kind of attention when I was growing up.

RENATA. Wait – what are you even saying? How is this even related?

CARIDAD. I was the black sheep – literally – the black sheep.

RENATA. Oh Cari, c'mon. That's such a terrible cop out –

CARIDAD. But it's true! Everyone preferred you, *ay qué nena tan bella*[1] you know? Even my own husband. It was disgusting. You know how hard that was?

RENATA. Is that why our relationship changed so much? We used to be close, Cari. I used to look up to you, you were like a second mother to me.

CARIDAD. I know, mija. I considered you my child too. I'm the one who named you! ...And I'm sorry about how I reacted after the whole thing. I regret it all the time. Honestly, I do.

RENATA. That hurt me. It still hurts...

CARIDAD. But I never blamed you. I never thought it was your fault.

RENATA. Because it wasn't! Like what the fuck did I do to warrant that kind of attention?

---

1. oh, what a beautiful girl

CARIDAD. Juan was a very sick man. But I just couldn't help but feel resentment. I was depressed, desperate… I had the kids…money was hard, I… You wouldn't understand…

RENATA. No, I think I do. It just…it didn't have to happen that way… we should have talked about it. This is what I mean – I had to take care of myself, console myself through that whole entire thing. I was only twelve. That wasn't fair.

CARIDAD. No, it wasn't fair. If I could take it all back I would. Pero what happened to you wasn't my fault either nena. And I never ever stopped loving you.

RENATA. I never blamed you either. I just felt very alone and it was fucked up.

CARIDAD. Lo siento, mija… But I did what I had to do. I got rid of him –

RENATA. I think I had enough of this conversation for now. Can we just –

CARIDAD. Sí, claro. *Ya, yo no quiero maldad en mi corazón. ¿Queires té de manzanilla?*[2]

> (**CARIDAD** *heads to the cupboard and takes out a tin can of dried chamomile flowers.*)

> (**RENATA** *nods her head yes.*)

> (*As* **CARIDAD** *says the following, she does all the steps in real time: picking the flowers, putting water into the pot, adding the honey, and squeezing the lemon.*)

Natural and organic is the best way. You pick the flowers from the earth that loved us first. And the love from your hands touches the plants, the honey, the lemon, the water… Your love stirs the mixture. And then when it's all done, your body drinks that love.

---

2. That's it. I don't want hate in my heart. Would you like some chamomile tea?

RENATA. Ahhh, so that's your secret ingredient huh?

CARIDAD. Passed down through "generations," mija.

(*She winks.*)

Believe in your strength, Renata. Have faith y la seguridad que nuestros ángeles están con nosotros.[1] Our ancestors guide us through our healing también. Do you pray at all? Light candles?

RENATA. I have an altar. It's not as elaborate as yours. Or how Mami's was.

CARIDAD. You do?! Well that's surprising. What's on it?

RENATA. Chakra candles, flowers, Sonia Sotomayor, a Buddha –

CARIDAD. A Buddha? You don't have a picture of Mami up there?

RENATA. I do...

CARIDAD. You should always light a candle for her.

RENATA. I light one for Papi too...

CARIDAD. *He needs many candles.*

RENATA. About Papi, great segue –

CARIDAD. *¡Espérate!* All this wine is making its way down.

(**CARIDAD** *gives the wooden spoon to* **RENATA**.)

Here, toss the meat and make yourself useful.

(*She rushes to the bathroom.*)

(**RENATA** *makes her way to the stove and tosses the meat around. She rubs her belly and talks to her unborn child.*)

---

1. and the security that our angels are with us.

RENATA. This might be good actually. Long overdue. What do you think, huh? Your titi is teaching me how to make you Boricua food. And we're actually *talking*. Nice, right? ...I know... She's not very nice. It's okay. She's got a lot of pent-up emotions. This is called grief, my baby. And we are a family. Not a perfect one, but a *familia* nonetheless.

Scene Three

Planted Seeds

(**RENATA** *and* **CARIDAD** *are at the table.* **RENATA** *passes the peeled yuca to* **CARIDAD**.)

(*First time jump – about twenty minutes.*)

RENATA. These are too hard to chop. I'm afraid I might piss on myself from all the force.

CARIDAD. Please don't piss in my kitchen. It's unsanitary... You know how to peel a plátano?

RENATA. No.

CARIDAD. Ay nena, what *do* you know?

RENATA. I know a lot of things actually.

CARIDAD. *No empieces –*[1]

RENATA. I got registered on that ancestry website.

CARIDAD. (*Surprised.*) You were able to find out things?

RENATA. Not much. But I did find a census report – Abuela was listed as a mulatta. Interesting, huh?

CARIDAD. Yep. Her father.

(**CARIDAD** *caresses her cheek.*)

RENATA. You kind of look like her.

CARIDAD. And I was always proud of it. Whenever Papi would criticize me and tell me I needed to be with a white man to *mejorar la raza*,[2] I'd just think about how beautiful Abuela was.

RENATA. He would tell you that?

CARIDAD. Papi's a racist, Rena. He didn't want his legacy to have any trace of brown in it –

---

1. Don't start
2. better the race

RENATA. Ay, please stop. We're Puerto Rican, Cari. Our family is all mixed and he was discriminated against too.

CARIDAD. So, you don't remember him telling you to straighten your hair?

(She does remember.)

RENATA. You know what else I found on that site? That Abuelo died in the second world war, death unknown. I found his draft card. He was drafted in his forties. Isn't that sad?

CARIDAD. Abuela always spoke about him. They were madly in love, *bendito...*

RENATA. Tell me about Abuela. Mami never really talked about her that much.

CARIDAD. Of course she did. You were just never around to hear it –

RENATA. Ey! ¡No empieces tú!

> (**CARIDAD** *grabs Abuela's mantilla that's on the altar.)*

CARIDAD. This was Abuela's... one of her favorite quotes was – *uno dice, pero Dios dispone...*

> *(She begins embodying Abuela, the living room space becomes the church.)*

She used to be a eucharistic minister at the church, one of the people who would go up to the altar and serve the communion. She was always so proud of that responsibility... I went to mass with her every Sunday.

Abuela never missed a misa. She's the one who taught me how to pray.

> *(She lights a candle from the altar. It glows.)*

CARIDAD. She taught me how to light the candles and how to set intention into them. We would walk around the entire iglesia and follow the stations of the cross. I used to stare into the stained glass windows showing God's seven days of creation…

> *(She takes the Virgin Mary statue that is on the altar and holds it in her hands.)*

She would point at the statues and teach me about the santos. She personally loved la Virgen María because she said she would visit her in dreams. She even claimed that one time la Virgen appeared to her in her little room where she slept, en el campo.

> *(A shadow of the Virgin Mary appears on the wall behind her.)*

Abuela was very poor growing up in Puerto Rico. She only made it to the second grade. But that woman was smart! She taught herself how to read and write. When she came to the states, she learned English on her own… She was *amazing*.

> *(She places the statue back, doing the sign of the cross.)*

Ay, and she loved to sing. She wasn't a great singer but she sang with heart. You could hear the faith in her voice. I can still hear it.

> *(As **CARIDAD** remembers Abuela, she hears a song as if it were being sung at church and sings a song in the style of "Entre Tus Manos" by Ray Repp.[1])*

---

1. A license to produce *Sancocho* does not include a performance license for "Entre Tus Manos." by Ray Repp. The publisher and author suggest that the licensee contact ASCAP or BMI to ascertain the music publisher and contact such music publisher to license or acquire permission for performance of the song. If a license or permission is unattainable for "Entre Tus Manos," the licensee may not use the song in *Sancocho* but should create an original composition in a similar style or use a similar song in the public domain. For further information, please see the Music and Third-Party Materials Use Note on page iii.

(**CARIDAD** *takes a moment to hear Abuela's voice. As she speaks the next few lines, she takes off the shawl, puts her apron back on, and reenters the kitchen.*)

Abuela was all that I had. Mami worked long hours during the week at the factory. Papi was...you know... He spent his days depressed. Playing his out-of-tune guitar, singing his sad boleros.

RENATA. He loves his boleros. I was thinking that we should probably be ready to hire a live band to sing old songs at his funeral. Like, "En Mi Viejo San Juan" and songs like that –

CARIDAD. Those boleros weren't cheerful moments, Rena. There were times I would run away and just live with Abuela for weeks, months. But Mami and Papi always came back to get me. And what could Abuela do? I was their kid. Not hers.

RENATA. You never tried to live with her when you were old enough?

CARIDAD. She passed three weeks before my eighteenth birthday...bendito. She was the best thing in my life. I miss her every day.

RENATA. She lives on through you, Cari.

(*A moment.*)

CARIDAD. So you've never peeled a plátano, eh?

RENATA. Nope.

CARIDAD. Go into the drawer and take out a knife with a sharp point.

RENATA. Do I really have to right now?

(**CARIDAD** *hands her the plátano.*)

CARIDAD. It's essential.

(**RENATA** *reluctantly searches in the silverware drawer.* **CARIDAD** *finishes making her tea.*)

RENATA. Okay, so like a utility knife?

CARIDAD. A *what*? Just grab a knife, my goodness.

(**RENATA** *keeps shuffling through the silverware.*)

RENATA. Why don't you have a knife block like every other normal person?!

CARIDAD. A knife block?! Ha! Maybe if you grew up with violent borrachos then you'd know how dangerous it is to keep things like that out in the open! Pero muchacha, you're looking through the wrong drawer!

(**RENATA** *has the utility knife in her hand and presents it like so:*)

RENATA. *And herein lies the multi-purpose utility knife in all of its glory.*

CARIDAD. Ay, yes whatever, that will work.

RENATA. So what do I do now?

CARIDAD. Slice off both ends of the plátano.

(**RENATA** *does.*)

Okay. Good. Now, you see how the banana has like edges all around it?

RENATA. Oh yeahhhh, it does.

CARIDAD. Now take the point of the knife and cut into the edge, try to make a clean slice from the top of that edge all the way down to the bottom. There are usually three edges, slice down all of them.

(*She does.*)

RENATA. Okay, what do I do now? Just peel it?

(She tries to peel one side of it off but it's tough and stays stuck on the banana.)

CARIDAD. No nena. It's not gonna peel off that easily. The cáscara is too thick –

Cut right into where you made the slice and get the *knife under the skin and peel it off*... Aha, así.[1] Bring the knife up towards you. But be careful. Don't cut yourself.

*(**RENATA** tries. She's kind of successful.)*

Keep trying, you'll get the hang of it. I didn't get it my first time either.

RENATA. How old were you?

CARIDAD. Eleven.

RENATA. You've been cooking since eleven? I didn't know you were that young.

CARIDAD. Someone had to make dinner for Papi while Mami was working...

(An awkward silence.)

RENATA. So umm...about that –

CARIDAD. What about that?

RENATA. Papi.

CARIDAD. What else do you want from me? I said do what you wish, *que no me importa*...[2] So tell me about Carlos. How's he preparing for fatherhood?

RENATA. You love changing the subject don't you?

CARIDAD. Because I already told you that I'm not interested in talking about Papi. I'm interested in *you*.

---

1. Yes, like that.
2. I don't care...

RENATA. *Really?*

CARIDAD. *Pero claro estúpida.*[1] If I wasn't interested, I wouldn't ask.

> (**RENATA** *sees the recao on the table and grabs it.*)

RENATA. So um...you want me to chop these?

CARIDAD. First of all, you don't *chop* recao. And no – we're not using that today.

RENATA. But I thought it was a necessary ingredient?

CARIDAD. Oh it is. Just not today...

> (**RENATA** *looks at her suspiciously.*)

RENATA. Should I even ask why?

CARIDAD. Not everybody likes recao.

RENATA. Who?

> (**CARIDAD** *continues chopping the yuca ignoring* **RENATA***'s follow-up question.*)

CARIDAD. So, Carlos?

RENATA. It's crazy but... Sometimes I feel like leaving him and just raising my daughter alone. I think I'd be a great single mom.

CARIDAD. No digas cosas así.[2] You think being a single mom is fun? Because let me tell you nena, it's NOT.

RENATA. You did it.

CARIDAD. That was a different time. They don't make women like me anymore.

RENATA. If you could do it, I could do it.

---

1. But of course, stupid.
2. Don't say things like that.

CARIDAD. I'm not saying it's impossible, but how would you be a single mom with the kind of career you have? Carlos is great, no sea ingrata.[3]

RENATA. I just thought that eventually he would grow up and mature. Doesn't everyone have to?

CARIDAD. No, Rena. Most men don't change. They're a very fixed kind of animal.

RENATA. Men are human beings. Just like us.

(**CARIDAD** *bursts out in laughter.*)

CARIDAD. Qué human beings?! You're too idealistic.

RENATA. I'm actually trying to be realistic here, Cari.

CARIDAD. Maybe he feels less of a man sometimes. I could imagine that to be the case. Especially being with *you*. You know, being a lawyer and all.

RENATA. Okay, now you're jumping into irrelevant shit. He's *proud* of me, alright? He knows how much I worked to get where I'm at.

CARIDAD. But you make more money than him.

RENATA. He has his own thing going on! Yeah I might make more than him, but he's a respected community organizer, CEO of his own non-profit that he built on his sweat and tears.

CARIDAD. ¡Y punto! ¿Ves?[4]

RENATA. What?

CARIDAD. That you're just never happy, Rena. You just defended your man for being this great and well-respected community activist / yet you put him down for being a bit immature.

---

3. don't be ungrateful
4. And point made! See?

RENATA. I never said he was a bad person!

CARIDAD. What has he done to be so immature? His dirty socks?

RENATA. I have to tell him something three times before he actually does it. He doesn't make his own dentist appointments. If I send him to the grocery store, he usually gets the wrong shit. I tell him to lay off the sweets, that diabetes runs in his family, but he doesn't listen to me. And I get worried you know? I don't need him to die prematurely because he doesn't care about his health! What about the baby? She deserves to have a father who will dance with her at her quinceñera and walk her down the aisle.

CARIDAD. Men don't care about their health, Rena. They never do.

RENATA. Ay Cari, that's just a biased generalization. I know plenty of men who are fifty years old and in their prime. You should see some of the guys I work with at the firm. They'll spend eight to ten hours at the office and then pick up their gym bags and go work out. These men buy salads for lunch.

CARIDAD. Look at Papi! Prime example of how men don't care about their health.

RENATA. That's what it is! I think about Papi and I don't want Carlos to end up like that.

CARIDAD. Carlos is nothing like Papi. Papi was a drunkard who ate lard-fried chicharron and abused everything he could get his hands on. Okay?

RENATA. Papi is laying on his deathbed right now. Have some sympathy –

CARIDAD. Sympathy! Ay, nena...if only you knew.

RENATA. What is it? If I only knew what? Tell me.

CARIDAD. Nothing.

(She drinks.)

RENATA. Oh, come on. If you're gonna talk shit, then just say the fucking shit!

CARIDAD. It's not fucking shit! You will never understand, Rena. You met Papi at a totally different time. There's a whole twenty plus years you don't know about that man.

RENATA. Like what?! Just tell me, Cari. Isn't that why you wanted me to stay? So we could talk. To, I don't know, get things out in the open? Well now it's your turn. What is it?

CARIDAD. ...

RENATA. What are you afraid of?

CARIDAD. You will never see him the same way again.

RENATA. And?

CARIDAD. I'm trying to protect you *idiota.*

RENATA. I'm not an idiot!

CARIDAD. Why would you want to hear terrifying things about a man who you've adored your whole life, huh? A man who's dying right now –

RENATA. You need to tell me what the hell it is that you're hiding from me!

CARIDAD. No. I don't.

RENATA. Everything. I want to know everything. I'm not fucking leaving until I know –

CARIDAD. Sometimes the truth is better not knowing.

RENATA. That's what I do for a living. Defend the truth!

CARIDAD. And you think I didn't spend my life *defending* everyone around me? Including you! That's all I've ever done and I didn't get paid for that mielda tampoco.[1] Not even a thank you!

---

1. shit, either – ("mielda" is Puerto Rican vernacular for "mierda.")

RENATA. I understand what you're saying, that's why I'm giving you the opportunity to speak your truth!

CARIDAD. It's just…very painful to unpack, nena.

(**CARIDAD** *drinks. She refills her glass.*)

RENATA. I heard about things, you know? But I just can't imagine him doing the things you and Mami said he did.

CARIDAD. Just because you can't imagine it doesn't make it untrue.

RENATA. He always said that with me he had a second chance to make things right. And you know what? He lived up to it. He was there for me, he believed in me, he encouraged me to be my best self whenever I felt like giving up. I'm sorry he wasn't that person for you. You know – this is why you need therapy too –

CARIDAD. No I don't. I don't believe in having to *pay* someone else to talk about your problems. That's all bullshit. To listen to someone else tell me shit I already know? To talk to some stranger about my personal life? No joda.[1]

RENATA. But you need to *unpack* all of this shit and forgive the man. Because he's gonna die and you're gonna miss your chance.

CARIDAD. HE missed that chance. He did a lot of unforgivable things.

(*The sound of a clock ticking is heard.* **CARIDAD** *hears the birds.*)

---

1. Stop messing around.

Scene Four

The Sun, Moon, and Star

(A moment later. **CARIDAD** *and* **RENATA** *are at the kitchen table.* **CARIDAD** *hands* **RENATA** *a yautía root to peel.)*

RENATA. Damn, another yam?!

CARIDAD. *Yautía...*

RENATA. *Mi tía?*

CARIDAD. Sí, peel it por favor. Another Taíno word by the way...

(**RENATA** *starts peeling.)*

RENATA. I know some Taíno words too – batey, cacique –

CARIDAD. You learned that in school?

RENATA. Ehhh, not really. I had to do my own research in college.

CARIDAD. Cuando yo era niña, I would go to the library and just read. It was how I eventually got my GED when I couldn't finish high school. Abuela used to always tell me there was nothing more important than an education. So, I made sure I studied. I'm self-taught too, you know? And proud of it.

RENATA. Why couldn't you finish high school?

CARIDAD. I had to work, Rena. Mami was having trouble with the bills and Papi was too drunk to hold down a job. This was after he lost the bodega.

RENATA. What kind of work did you do?

(**CARIDAD** *pours herself the last bit of wine that's left in the bottle.)*

CARIDAD. Odd jobs here and there.

RENATA. Damn, you finished that whole bottle by yourself?

CARIDAD. Oh please, real women drink full bottles of wine.

RENATA. Said no one, ever.

CARIDAD. I don't know…maybe if you google it you'll find a study on it.

RENATA. If I google it, I'd find pages like "if you're able to drink a whole bottle of wine to the head then you might be an alcoholic."

CARIDAD. Look who's criticizing who now.

RENATA. I'm just telling it like how I see it.

CARIDAD. After you peel the yautía, make sure you cut them in fourths.

RENATA. Got it.

>   (**RENATA** *continues peeling.* **CARIDAD** *takes off her apron and starts tidying up the living room.*)

What are you doing?

CARIDAD. Nada. Just tidying the place up a bit.

RENATA. Why do you keep acting so strange?

CARIDAD. You're the one making it strange. I'm just doing what I always do.

RENATA. Uh-huh.

>   (*She continues peeling.*)

CARIDAD. Keep coming back to learn how to cook and I guarantee you Carlos will be healthy. Instead of him buying the sweets, you can make the sweets. Use all of that *organic* stuff you love and monitor how much sugar goes into it.

RENATA. Ay Cari, who the hell has time for that?!

CARIDAD. ¿Y tu hija?[1] You gonna feed her that porquería[2] they sell in the supermarkets?

RENATA. They got healthy options these days, Caridad. Don't be such a *jíbara*.[3]

> (**RENATA** *starts chopping the yautía.*)

CARIDAD. Excuse you, but you said earlier – that you wanted to be wholesome. *Papitas con huevos frito.*[4] That's *jíbaro* food, okay? And I'm proud to be a *jíbara*. You talk all this shit and disregard the fact that that's what you come from.

RENATA. It's just a figure of speech.

CARIDAD. To you it is.

> (**CARIDAD** *looks at the time.*)

What's in Papi's will, anyway? That *jíbaro*.

RENATA. Seriously?

CARIDAD. Yes. I'm ready to talk about it now.

RENATA. Why all of a sudden?

CARIDAD. Because. It's getting late, no?

RENATA. Late for what? I thought you wanted me to stay –

CARIDAD. Stop with the fucking interrogation Renata. We're not in the damn courtroom!

RENATA. I just think it's suspicious that you look at the time and all of a sudden you wanna talk about Papi's will because it's getting *late*?

---

1. And your daughter?
2. bullshit
3. hick/hillbilly
4. french fries with fried eggs

CARIDAD. Who you think this big ass pot of sancocho is for? Just you and me?

RENATA. *(Super sarcastic.)* Oh, right...it's *Sunday*. So, who's coming to dinner?

CARIDAD. Sergio and Lydia. So, what is the bastard leaving behind? / What other secrets did he have?

RENATA. / Cari, have some respect! ...Wait, secrets?

CARIDAD. Secret assets? Did he have any assets?

RENATA. I mean he has that old '65 Mustang that's rusting in my garage.

CARIDAD. Worthless piece of metal.

RENATA. Actually, Carlos says if we fix it up it could be worth like twenty thousand dollars. Maybe more, who knows?

CARIDAD. Yeah uh huh, after how much you gotta spend to fix it?

RENATA. I don't know about cars...

CARIDAD. Ask your nephew Sergio. ¿Qué mas? What else he got?

RENATA. I don't like your tone, Cari. It sounds –

CARIDAD. ¿Cómo que?[1] What I sound like now?

(She drinks.)

RENATA. I don't know, it's aggressive. Please stop / drinking.

CARIDAD. / Because I don't really care about what that viejo has to leave, I want nothing of it! I was only asking because maybe for once in his pathetic life he could leave something of value behind.

RENATA. Well before he got really sick I made sure that he took out a good life insurance plan. I paid for it myself mostly – you know the monthly payments.

---

1. Like how?

CARIDAD. ¿Y?

RENATA. I mean after funeral costs and all that –

CARIDAD. We should just cremate him. Let him burn.

(*She drinks.*)

RENATA. *Let him burn?* What the fuck is wrong with you?

CARIDAD. What?! It's a thing! People get cremated! They want their ashes scattered across some fucking mountain they've never been able to climb! It's cheaper too, you know?

RENATA. No he wants to be in a mausoleum –

CARIDAD. He does NOT deserve to be peacefully laying up in some wall!

RENATA. Well he's my father too Cari, and I love him and that's what he wants so that's what he's gonna get!

(**CARIDAD** *mocks her.*)

CARIDAD. *Oooh, he's my daddy, and I love him and he always preferred me because I was the one who came out light-skinned with pretty eyes...* Papi just loved you so much didn't he?!

RENATA. Why is it so hard for you to believe that people can actually change? He didn't *prefer* me because I came out white okay? / He was just at a different place in his life.

CARIDAD. / Yes he did! You were worthy to him and he believed in you. He was a self-hating prick! He called me bemba, said all I was good for was for working and rearing babies. He never forgave me for being the one who lived!

RENATA. Are you talking about your twin?

CARIDAD. Sí nena. You know the story –

RENATA. He was beautiful...*with blonde hair and blue eyes.*

CARIDAD. Took after Papi's side. When that baby died, Papi was apparently never the same. I always felt like he resented me for that.

RENATA. Don't say that, Cari. You were just a baby, that's not right.

CARIDAD. Pero, it's true! I came out brown. He was disappointed with me from the very beginning. *Siempre buscando lo que no tenía…*[1]

RENATA. Do you think the baby died of SIDS?

CARIDAD. I don't know what happened, bendito. He was sick. Back then, if you were sick and Puerto Rican, that was a common thing.

RENATA. Poor Mami. That must have been so hard.

CARIDAD. Sí nena, ella sufrió mucho.[2]

RENATA. I can't imagine losing a child.

CARIDAD. You don't know how good you had it.

RENATA. How *good* I had it?

CARIDAD. You didn't have to justify your existence like I did.

RENATA. You must have not been aware of all the pressure I endured while growing up! The pressure of having to succeed, being the one that the family could later rely on. I put my own ass through law school! Wanna know why?! Because we were poor, and I knew that I had to make money in order for us to be good in the future! If it weren't for me, Mami would've never died peacefully in a beautiful place! I did that! I worked for that! I'm still paying for that!

CARIDAD. Why did you feel you had to take up that burden?! I spent my whole life caring for my parents! All I've done in my life is serve, serve, serve and fucking serve! And all anyone ever did was take and take and take!

---

1. Always looking for what he didn't have…
2. Yes nena, she suffered a lot.

RENATA. Stop saying that. That's not true at all –

CARIDAD. How the fuck would you know! Now you're lighting my gas!

> (**CARIDAD** *moves over to the stove and continues to toss around the meat, lowering the flame and adding a bit more water. It's all love on that stove. She looks at the time again.*)

So, you said after all the funeral costs and the fucking mausoleum...?

RENATA. There's gonna be fifty thousand dollars we are going to have to split.

> (**CARIDAD** *drops her tongs.*)

CARIDAD. What?

RENATA. Fifty thousand dollars.

CARIDAD. This is after the fucking mausoleum?

RENATA. Bomba! How you like that?

CARIDAD. That's a lot of money, Renata. How the fuck did he get a hold of all that money?

RENATA. His life insurance...and you're not gonna believe this...but he won a lot of money playing those underground lottery games.

CARIDAD. Sí, los numeros...[3]

> (*She sits down in awe.*)

RENATA. So now can we finally have this conversation?

> (**CARIDAD** *chugs down her wine. It's the end of that glass.*)

CARIDAD. Qué mierda.[4] I need more wine.

---

3. Right, the numbers.
4. Shit.

RENATA. No you don't!

CARIDAD. YES. I. Do.

Scene Five

Flying Sea Creatures

(*CARIDAD opens the fridge and pops open a bottle of white wine that has been chilling.*)

RENATA. You're switching over to white now?

CARIDAD. Wine is wine. It's all the same fucking shit.

(*She pours herself a glass.*)

You want one?

RENATA. I can't Cari.

CARIDAD. Ay, you can have one. Pregnant women do it all the time. Google it.

RENATA. No, I'm good. Knock yourself out.

CARIDAD. Start peeling the corn. Please.

(**RENATA** *grabs the corn and starts peeling off the husks.*)

There's something I gotta tell you…

(**CARIDAD** *starts pacing around the kitchen.*)

RENATA. What?

CARIDAD. I didn't know Papi was leaving money.

RENATA. That's why you shoulda looked at those documents when I told you to –

CARIDAD. There's a lot to consider now… This whole inheritance thing we are dealing with is about to get really tricky.

RENATA. Don't worry. Papi's lawyer is a good colleague of mine and knows what he's doing –

CARIDAD. No, you don't get it.

(**CARIDAD** *sips.*)

RENATA. Look, I'm a professional. Let me do what I do best. As his proxy, I made sure his lawyer drafted a will that's fair, clear, and honest. Our situation isn't that complicated. It's just us – you and me. We split everything he leaves behind. It's all equal. We just gotta figure out what to do with that Mustang.

(*A beat.*)

CARIDAD. What if it's not just us?

RENATA. You mean Sergio and Lydia? –

CARIDAD. No. I mean, we have a brother.

RENATA. The baby who died?

CARIDAD. No. Not him. Que en paz descanse.

RENATA. So then who the hell are you talking about?

CARIDAD. Papi had another son. *After* me.

RENATA. He. WHAT?! Have you lost your mind?

CARIDAD. Your loving and innocent father had an extramarital affair and we have *another brother*. You have an older brother.

RENATA. You're fucking lying. Stop shitting me.

CARIDAD. Oh I wish I was.

(**RENATA** *is in shock.* **CARIDAD** *drinks.*)

RENATA. This is a really big fucking secret, Cari! A big accusation! Are you sure about this!?

CARIDAD. Sure of it like the pelitos[1] on my chin. This is what death brings, mija – a whole bunch of secrets.

---

1. little hairs

RENATA. Well how the fuck do YOU know about it?

CARIDAD. I was pretty young, but I remember it like it was yesterday. She called the house, the mistress, and Mami picked up the phone and just broke down. But then, *la chilla*[2] *ésa* sent a letter in the mail with a picture of a boy, spitting image of Papi. Mami ripped up that letter, she didn't want Papi finding out. He always wanted a son, so she thought that he would go run off and abandon us. Papi had the bodega at the time and Mami was really counting on his income. This was when her arthritis began to act up, so she couldn't do the factory as often.

RENATA. But if she ripped it all up then how –

CARIDAD. I was a kid, Rena. I was curious. So I found the letter and the photo in the trash and taped it back together. I kept in touch with him for a little while, but then years passed by –

RENATA. What about the other woman?

CARIDAD. Well the reason why she sent that stuff was because she had cancer and wanted her son to know who his father was.

RENATA. Did Papi ever know about him?

CARIDAD. After Mami found out that I knew I promised her I would never tell. But –

RENATA. How old is he now?

CARIDAD. He's fifty-five or fifty-six. He's a history teacher. Nice guy.

RENATA. Oh my God... I literally cannot fucking believe this.

CARIDAD. *Ay nena...la vida es un carnaval.*[3]

RENATA. What's his name?

---

2. the mistress/side chick
3. Oh girl...life is a carnival.

CARIDAD. Eduardo García De Jesús.

RENATA. He's a De Jesús?!

CARIDAD. Yup. Eddie's mother gave him Papi's last name.

RENATA. Why are you telling me this *now*? Don't you think this is something you should have fucking told me about a long ass time ago?!

CARIDAD. Well – I was waiting for the *right time* actually –

RENATA. No! There's no "right time." And honestly – you picked the worst fucking *time* to say anything! I cannot believe this, this is –

CARIDAD. Locura. Sí, I know. Now there's a will, and there's money –

RENATA. What are you suggesting we do? Include him in the will? I don't even fucking know him.

CARIDAD. I don't know but we gotta do something, Rena. I gotta do something.

RENATA. You want me to just call him up and be like, "Hey Eddie, it's your sister Renata who you've never met – you don't mind that I call you Eddie? – Okay, great! Well Eddie, Papi died, the guy you never met, and uh, here's $16k... are you interested in a Mustang?"

CARIDAD. I don't know what we should do, Renata! He was abandoned. Lived a hard life because Papi couldn't man up to his responsibility. And now that Papi has this money he's leaving, it only seems right to give Eddie some kind of reparation –

RENATA. Don't be hysterical! Papi didn't even know about him. For all he knew, there was no baby from that affair. There's gonna be a will that won't have his name on it.

CARIDAD. That just sounds immoral.

RENATA. You wanna talk ethics now?

CARIDAD. Papi knows.

RENATA. What you mean Papi knows?

> (**CARIDAD** *chops the corncobs into halves. It's loud and the silence around the chopping is even louder.*)

Hello??? What do you mean by "Papi knows," Cari?

CARIDAD. Hold on.

> (*She adds water to the pot, raising the flame high to get a nice boil. She gathers all the vegetables: corn, carrots, potatoes, yuca, and yautía and puts them to the side. She heads to the fridge and takes out a jar full of liquid. She adds it to the water.*)

RENATA. Oh my God, give me patience please. Give me strength.

CARIDAD. Vegetable broth...

> (*She heads towards the spice rack.*)

Bay leaves and a cubito[1] of beef bouillon.

> (**CARIDAD** *stirs. It's magic again.* **RENATA** *is mesmerized for a moment.* **CARIDAD** *stays near the stove waiting for the water to boil.*)

RENATA. So. Tell me about Eddie.

CARIDAD. Eduardo grew up as a bastard child with a single mother. She passed away from cancer when he was twelve years old. He had nobody. His mother was an immigrant, I think from Colombia. She had no family in the U.S. Not that we knew of. So when she died, he was sent to foster care and went from home to home until he was eighteen. He would write to me all the time, bendito. He was so lonely.

RENATA. What, now you guys were pen pals or something?

---

1. cube

CARIDAD. No, we used to write to each other.

*(That went over **RENATA**'s head.)*

RENATA. Did he have an alias? How did he send you letters with no one catching on?

CARIDAD. Alias? No estúpida –

RENATA. Hey! Watch your / tongue please.

CARIDAD. / No alias! Nothing like that. He would use his name, Eddie García. That's what he normally goes by. Legally he's a De Jesús, it's on his birth certificate I'm sure.

RENATA. So you wrote each other letters all the time? What did you two write about?

CARIDAD. He wanted someone keeping track of him. He would sometimes get abused at the homes he would live in. They would steal his checks and sometimes I would send him money... it was really really ugly, Rena. I don't wanna talk about it...

RENATA. You need to tell me. You need to talk... So, you wrote letters to each other?

CARIDAD. He would write to me and tell me about his dreams, bendito. He used to have these big dreams. Him and I used to dream a lot, we would have lucid dreams. You know, like those dreams when you have money in your hands and it feels so real?

RENATA. And then you wake up and your hand is empty! And then you're like, fuck man!!

CARIDAD. Yes! It's such a terrible feeling! ...Ay, and we had like a little book club. Eddie's the one who recommended, *One Hundred Years of Solitude*... it's how I fell in love with the name Renata. And in his soledad, Eddie was swept away by the magic of Gabriel García Márquez.

RENATA. That's...*ironically beautiful*, but I don't get it Cari. How could you have had this relationship with him? Where was he?

CARIDAD. He would occasionally be sent to a foster home that was close to where we lived and we would meet up at the library.

RENATA. How long did this even go on?

CARIDAD. It lasted for years. Abuela knew about him too.

RENATA. Abuela knew?! I guess it wasn't her place to say anything.

CARIDAD. She didn't get involved with Mami and Papi's affairs.

RENATA. So how did Papi find out?

CARIDAD. He showed up once.

RENATA. He did?! When?!

CARIDAD. Ay nena, this was casi forty years ago. It was a total surprise too. It looked like he made the decision on a whim. He was always thinking about how he would meet Papi, you know, uno siempre quiere conocer a su padre...[1]

RENATA. Okay – So...Eddie showed up one day and the jig was up?

CARIDAD. Yeah. One day I'm home cooking. Mami wasn't home, thank God. And the buzzer rings. A familiar ring, though... You know how Mami always pressed the *timbre* twice –

RENATA. Two times real fast!

CARIDAD & RENATA. Beep Beep!

---

1. One always wants to know who their parent is...

CARIDAD. Yup! That's how you knew it was Mami! And Abuela would just hold it down for a long time, like beeeeeeeeeeeep. That's how you knew it was Abuela. Even after you would buzz her in, she'd keep her finger on the button. We would have to yell out the window, "¡Ya Abuela! ¡Entra!"[1] Pero, this time the timbre sounded the way that Papi would ring it. Así como...[2]

CARIDAD & RENATA. Beeeeeeep. Beep. Beep. Beep.

CARIDAD. Yeah. And Eddie rang the bell just like that. Con el mismo ritmo.[3] And of course this was weird – Papi was in the other room watching la noticias[4] so it wasn't him. And I remember this creepy feeling, goosebumps on my skin. Y lo sabía.[5] You know? I just knew it was Eddie. My heart was pumping so hard and so fast that I thought it was showing from my chest. And then I heard Papi yelling out, "¡¿Quién está en la puerta?!"[6] It was as if he knew something was up too. Papi had what you call the sixth sense?

RENATA. That's true. He could always predict things too.

CARIDAD. That's right. Before I even knew I was pregnant, Papi looked at me one day and told me, "Estás encinta con gemelos."[7] One month later I missed my period. Nine months later I had Sergio and Lydia.

RENATA. Before I started showing, he knew I was going to have a girl.

CARIDAD. So yeah, he knew something was up, and I knew something was up, and someone must've let Eddie inside the building because I heard footsteps coming up...

---

1. Enough, Abuela! Enter!
2. Like that, like...
3. With the same rhythm.
4. the news
5. And I just knew it.
6. Who's at the door?!
7. You're pregnant with twins.

(The sound of echoing footsteps is heard. **CARIDAD** *looks over to the side of the stage that has the altar. She looks towards the "door.")*

And at this point I'm shaking. I started having a cold sweat. Like a fever or something. He knocked on the door. It was such a light knock that it confused me. It didn't sound like the knock of a sixteen-year-old. Sounded more like a little kid with a tiny hand. And so I looked through the peephole thinking maybe it was just a child, but no – it was Eddie.

Knocking like a child...

(A light knock is heard on the door. **CARIDAD** *looks over at it.* **RENATA** *does not hear the knock.)*

I could hear him breathing on the other side. He was nervous. He didn't look well. He was breathing a little too hard. So I whispered to him from the other side of the door, I tell him, "Mira, Eddie, I'm gonna let you in, but you have to promise me you'll keep it down and not act up." ...And he tells me "I promise, I promise." At this point me estoy cagando[8] but it was hot outside and I could tell he needed water so I opened the door.

(The creak of the door opening is heard. She "sees" him collapse on the couch.)

And ay bendito. I will never forget that face he had. He collapsed on the sofa, sweating, I thought maybe he had been running away from someone. I offered him some water but he refused it. I was like, "Eddie, que te pasa?" And he wouldn't respond to me. Then all of a sudden I see Eddie stand up and he's looking behind me, scared, as if he was seeing a ghost. I turn around and it's Papi. And they were just standing there. Same

---

8. I'm shitting myself

height. Same eyes. Staring back at each other. Like a mirror. Eddie ran out of the apartment and Papi went back into his room and slammed the door.

RENATA. What do you think was going on with Eddie?

CARIDAD. He was into drugs at the time. Hard stuff. You know?

RENATA. And Papi put two and two together.

CARIDAD. Pero claro. He saw his own face standing there before him!

RENATA. He's known about Eddie all this time.

CARIDAD. Yes...and Mami got the beating of her life that night.

> *(She gulps down her wine and refills her glass.)*

And I did too. That's when I left that apartment for good.

> *(She heads back to the stove. She stirs. It's magic again. She lowers the flame and covers the pot.)*

Esa noche infame[1]...the devil himself possessed Papi.

RENATA. I...I can't believe it, this is confusing, I'm –

CARIDAD. It's a lot to take in. Do you want that glass of wine now?

RENATA. NO!

> **(CARIDAD** *takes a seat next to* **RENATA.***)*

CARIDAD. Bueno sí, aquí estamos[2]...

RENATA. I don't get it, why would Papi keep this from me?

---

1. That infamous night
2. Well, yes, here we are now...

CARIDAD. Don't be stupid! To keep himself looking like the perfect little daddy in his / perfect little daughter's eyes!

RENATA. / Do you think that if he could talk right now that he would tell me about Eddie?

CARIDAD. Doubt it.

RENATA. What if I bring it up to him? He can't speak much but that doesn't mean he's incoherent. He can blink his eyes once for no and twice for yes.

CARIDAD. He can do that?

RENATA. Yeah, maybe if you visited him more often you could see it for yourself.

CARIDAD. No. I don't want to see him like that. Seeing him all weak and vulnerable would make me just pity him. That man doesn't deserve an ounce of pity from me.

RENATA. Look I know that in his younger years he was abusive, but as he got older, he changed –

CARIDAD. *(Angry.)* No, he didn't change! He got weaker, yes, but he didn't change! He had a stroke and became immobile and needed us to wipe his fucking ass, but he didn't change! He still called Mami una hija de la gran puta[3] while you were in school! When she started losing her memory, he would lie to her and manipulate her! He didn't fucking change!

RENATA. Can you calm down, please?

CARIDAD. I am CALM!

> (**CARIDAD** *takes another sip of her wine. She makes her way to the stove. Stirring again. No anger on the stove. Just love. It's magic.)*

---

3. daughter of a bitch

RENATA. Now that I know that Papi knew about him, the only conclusion that I can make is that he doesn't claim Eddie as his son. It won't be fair to Papi if we put Eddie on his will, not without his permission. It would be wrong.

CARIDAD. Are you kidding me, Rena?! After everything I just told you? What do you need Papi's permission for, you're his proxy! It's not like he can call you out for it.

RENATA. No that would be *illegal.* Do you even know where Eddie is? How do we even contact him?

CARIDAD. I can find him.

RENATA. What do you mean you can find him?

CARIDAD. Well I know where he works. It's such a small world that one day I was dropping off some lunch to Sergio, at his car wash, and Eddie was there getting the inside of his car cleaned!

RENATA. Oh my God, really?

CARIDAD. I kid you not! And I see Eddie, and I'm like – "Eddie?!" It was kind of awkward, Sergio bugged me about it for months. He thought Eddie was an old boyfriend or something. But you know, we talked for a bit. That's when he told me about the school he was working at.

RENATA. Okay, but how long ago was this?

CARIDAD. I don't think he's retired yet. Don't you have to be like sixty years old to retire?

RENATA. It depends Cari… it depends if he's still even teaching there. When did he tell you this?

CARIDAD. I'm pretty sure he still works there.

RENATA. What do you know, Cari…

CARIDAD. Out of curiosity I walked passed the high school / recently to see if I would see him and I did.

RENATA. / I freaking knew it. How recent was this? Were you stalking him?

CARIDAD. No I wasn't stalking. Just watching.

RENATA. WHEN CARI?

CARIDAD. Last week.

RENATA. You creep! Why were you *watching* him?

CARIDAD. Because I know Papi is dying and I think Eddie should know! I just wanted to make sure that I could know where to find him when the time came...

RENATA. Okay, well... I don't know what to think, Cari. I'll ask Papi about it.

CARIDAD. He's never going to claim Eddie as his son, Renata! Don't be such a tonta, Dios mio! He's a fucking coward! I can't believe you think a *blink* is gonna solve everything. What kind of lawyer / are you?

RENATA. The kind of lawyer who adheres to the law! I can't just override his decisions, he's still coherent enough to make choices –

CARIDAD. He's dying Renata. He made you his proxy – that means YOU get to decide –

RENATA. Well he's not dead yet! Why are you so fixated on this? I told you I would ask Papi. That's enough!

CARIDAD. Eddie went through hell because your pendejo of a father was too proud to help out his only son... He saw Eddie suffering that day. He saw that Eddie was using. And he didn't care. He didn't do shit but beat me and Mami up for it!

RENATA. I hear you. But it's Papi's money, Cari. Not ours.

CARIDAD. You're a sellout.

RENATA. No I'm not! This isn't one of your courtroom dramas on TV, Cari /

CARIDAD. / You just don't wanna do it, eso es.

RENATA. Its a major decision – there's money on the line, phone calls to be made, paperwork to complete, percentages to figure out – this is not just something that gets done in one – two – three.

>   (**CARIDAD** *takes a moment to respond. Maybe she's surprised that she wasn't able to sway* **RENATA** *as quickly as she thought she would.*)

CARIDAD. Timing is everything, mija. Don't take it for granted while you still have it.

RENATA. I'm very aware of it, Cari.

CARIDAD. Pues, 'tá bien.[1]

>   (*The birds sing again.* **RENATA** *doesn't hear them, but* **CARIDAD** *does, and they are loud.*)

---

1. Well, fine then.

Scene Six

In God's Image

(**CARIDAD** *checks the stove. She stirs. It's magic again. She reaches for the radio, tuning it until she finds the right station that's playing salsa.[2] It's a nice slow salsa, a soulful one.* **CARIDAD** *drinks her wine. She's dancing.*)

(**RENATA** *looks at her. Forgiveness fills the air. Memories of a good time enter the room. When people truly adore each other, they can fight and then pretend nothing happened just seconds later... Who knows why this is so. But this is how Puerto Ricans are.*)

CARIDAD. ¡Levántate! Get up and dance with me! Life's too short to be moping around. Yeah, maybe you just found out about a brother you never thought you always had, but just dance it off, nena! Dance it off!

RENATA. Nope. I don't dance salsa.

CARIDAD. What you mean you don't dance salsa?! Of course you dance salsa!

RENATA. I only dance the easy stuff – merengue y bachata.

CARIDAD. Oh come on! It's easy.

RENATA. Salsa is hard, what are you talking about?

CARIDAD. What are YOU talking about? This is that "Boricua-kitchen" salsa baby, it's in your blood.

---

2. A license to produce *Sancocho* does not include a performance license for any third-party or copyrighted music. Licensees should create an original composition or use music in the public domain. For further information, please see the Music and Third-Party Materials Use Note on page iii.

(**RENATA** *stands up. They stand side by side together.* **CARIDAD** *slows down her steps.* **RENATA** *follows.)*

CARIDAD.　One–two–three, five–six–seven… One–two–three, five–six–seven… One–two–three, five–six–seven… así… you got it!

(*They're in sync. Perhaps* **RENATA** *was bluffing – maybe she was a bit rusty at first, but the woman can move.)*

CARIDAD & RENATA.　One–two–three, five–six–seven… One–two–three, five–six–seven… One–two–three, five–six–seven…

(**CARIDAD** *is dancing masterfully, she grabs* **RENATA** *and leads her.* **CARIDAD** *turns* **RENATA**, *and* **RENATA** *spins with grace. They dance for a bit. Let them have some fun.)*

(*A few moments later, they sit down to catch their breaths.* **CARIDAD** *refills her glass and drinks.)*

RENATA.　I think I'm gonna do it.

CARIDAD.　You gonna put Eddie on the will?

RENATA.　No – I'm not talking about that right now. That's for a whole other day.

CARIDAD.　So what the hell do you think you're gonna do?

RENATA.　Divorce Carlos.

(**CARIDAD** *spits out her wine.)*

CARIDAD.　¡¿Qué?!

RENATA.　Like you just said…life is too short. And I have this deep loud desire to be with someone that I absolutely adore.

CARIDAD. Ay nena, ¿qué te pasa ahora?[1]

RENATA. I'm just afraid that maybe I settled with someone who is more like a best friend. Carlos doesn't *access* all of me.

CARIDAD. No one is ever going to *access* all of you. You haven't even accessed all of yourself yet, mija. Wait until you actually become a mother. You'll see.

RENATA. I've seen other people so in love, am I wrong for wanting that too?

CARIDAD. Maybe you guys need to take a vacation somewhere and have some really awesome sex.

RENATA. Okay, Cari. I don't wanna talk about sex with you. Let's just drop it. Thanks.

CARIDAD. People are having these honeymoons for babies now! Spice it up a bit. Take a vacation from your problems.

RENATA. Vacations are just quick getaways... you come right back to the same problems.

CARIDAD. Ayyy, you're no fun.

(She fills her glass with more wine.)

RENATA. And in just about one more glass you will no longer be any fun... why the hell are you drinking so much tonight, huh? What's going on?

CARIDAD. I think you're pregnant –

RENATA. No shit –

CARIDAD. – And so you're feeling a lot of things. Which are valid. But right now you need to ride it out with Carlos. He is someone who loves you and who you can depend on.

---

1. What's wrong with you now?

(**CARIDAD** *grabs the grater and begins her grating-plátano process.*)

RENATA. I guess I just expected him to man up more. You know? Like, we're having a baby, *together* – but I feel like I'm alone in this journey. I can't *even* imagine him cleaning diapers.

CARIDAD. I'm sorry nena, but some men are just not good at that part. Doesn't mean that they won't be a good father, though. Anyways, you got me. Okay? *No te preocupes.*[1]

(*This sits right with* **RENATA**.)

RENATA. What about your mister right?

CARIDAD. Ha! That ship has sailed and reached other shores... you're still young. Anything is still possible.

RENATA. I just wish I didn't feel this way. It's fucked up right?

CARIDAD. No, it's okay to have doubts. It's a big commitment to have a child with someone. So yeah...maybe you just got cold feet.

RENATA. And here I thought cold feet only happens on your wedding night.

CARIDAD. A lot of things in this world will make your feet cold.

(**CARIDAD** *continues grating the plátano.*)

RENATA. What are you gonna do with that plátano?

CARIDAD. Roll them up into bolitas[2] so we drop them into the soup later as it's cooking. It's delicious.

RENATA. Damn, how many things do you gotta put in the sancocho?

---

1. Don't worry.
2. mini balls

CARIDAD. A lot. Why you think it takes so long?

(**CARIDAD** *continues grating.*)

(*Renata's phone rings loudly and interrupts their moment.*)

Carajo that scared the crap out of me!

(**RENATA** *picks up the phone.*)

RENATA. Hello? Hi, yes... this is she... hold on, please.

(**RENATA** *continues the call outside of the kitchen. The birds start singing again.* **CARIDAD** *takes in a deep breath and opens the kitchen window. A breeze flows through the curtains. She looks out the window and then closes her eyes, as if praying.*)

(**RENATA** *enters. She's cold. She's stiff. She sits down. She's silent.* **CARIDAD** *notices and takes a long good look at her.*)

CARIDAD. He's dead.

RENATA. Yes.

CARIDAD. I knew it.

RENATA. You did?

CARIDAD. I did.

RENATA. How long have you known?

CARIDAD. All day... since I was kid I knew about these things. I knew when it was Abuela. I knew when it was Mami... I would hear birds sing – the songs that the red cardinals sing – like right inside of my head...

(**RENATA** *cries. A moment, that might feel like forever.*)

RENATA. I... I... I just saw him... I saw him earlier Cari... and like... I didn't know... I didn't know it was gonna be the last time I was gonna see him... I... I barely said goodbye!

CARIDAD. Ay, Rena... you / didn't know mija.

RENATA. / I was in a rush, I had to rush over to see another client and I remember looking at the time and I saw that I was running out of time but I guess I didn't realize that I was actually running out of time and I ran out of there not even considering that it would be the last time I would fucking see Papi!

(**CARIDAD** *tries her best to console her.*)

CARIDAD. It's okay... ya... ya... no llores[1] mija... this is a part of life. You have survived it before and you will survive it again...

(*They grieve.*)

RENATA. That's it. He's gone.

CARIDAD. Yeah.

RENATA. Mami and Papi. Gone.

CARIDAD. Mmmhmm.

RENATA. My child won't know her grandparents. She won't ever meet Mami and Papi.

CARIDAD. It's okay.

RENATA. It's gonna have to be okay.

CARIDAD. It will be...

RENATA. So what do we do?

CARIDAD. What do you mean what do we do? We have to do what we need to do.

---

1. don't cry

*(**CARIDAD** gulps down her wine.)*

RENATA. I'm literally an orphan.

CARIDAD. Oh please, you're thirty-three years old.

RENATA. You're not sad at all?

CARIDAD. Of course I'm sad. Didn't you just see me cry with you?

RENATA. Yeah that was like a protocol cry. Like you know, how you're supposed to cry from the shock. Or whatever.

CARIDAD. *¡¿Ay qué shock ni qué shock?!* He was in pain for so long.

RENATA. You seem relieved.

CARIDAD. I am relieved.

RENATA. I get it. At least he's not in pain anymore.

CARIDAD. Ay nena, you feel bad for his pain, but the way I see it, it was his penance.

RENATA. That's not fair, don't say that –

CARIDAD. I don't expect you to understand what I am about to say, because unless you lived it, you will never ever really know...but Papi was Mami's villain. He was scared of her power.

Scared of her strength. He was scared of her ability to love. He was afraid that she could control him...and he put her through hell for his insecurity. Sometimes at night – when I can't shut off my brain – I think about how lucky Mami was to have had Alzheimer's in the end. That hopefully she forgot about all of the nasty and ugly shit...

RENATA. You really feel that way? I don't know, Cari. She was miserable.

CARIDAD. That if she happened to remember anything at all, I used to hope that God would be gracious and reward her with the good memories... There were a few...

RENATA. I think God granted her that because she died with a smile on her face.

CARIDAD. She really was smiling. I remember that vividly. Que Dios me la bendiga...[1]

RENATA. There were times when I saw Papi snap at Mami and I would act like it was all good but then I would go to bed thinking about how – no that shit wasn't all good...you know? Like I felt the embarrassment that Mami would feel. I would watch her shrink under him sometimes. And like, he didn't even have to hit her for anyone to feel the impact. By that time, they just had a way of being and I regretfully accepted it... And there were times that I was mean to him Cari... I was very mean to him sometimes.

CARIDAD. Well maybe you were life's revenge...

RENATA. Remember my third birthday?!

CARIDAD. Oh my God, of course I remember that day. I was recording the video!

RENATA. You guys were singing "Happy Birthday" to me and I yelled at him, for no reason, I was like, "No, Papi, you don't sing. I don't like you!"

CARIDAD. Yeah, that was weird. Everyone thought that was weird. I remember he was hurt by it too.

RENATA. That's my point... as I grew up I always had those feelings of spite. And I could never explain them because he was always so kind and generous to me.

CARIDAD. Pues sí, mija, así es la vida...[2]

---

1. May God bless her...
2. Well yes, love, that's how life is...

(She drinks more.)

RENATA. We need to go see his body, visit the nursing home –

CARIDAD. Let him rest in peace. We'll see his body tomorrow. Besides, he's with us right now.

(The birds sing again, a somber, but uplifting melody.)

Scene Seven

A Holy Day of Rest

> (**CARIDAD** *is stirring.* **RENATA** *is now pacing back and forth, cramping and doing breathing and stretching exercises.*)

RENATA. I say we call him.

CARIDAD. Call Eddie? And how do you suppose we do that?

RENATA. Oh c'mon I know you have his number somewhere. You're not a half-assed stalker. You go all in.

CARIDAD. Maybe a twenty on black at the roulette table, pero Rena, I do have some discipline!

RENATA. So you really don't have his number?!

CARIDAD. No.

RENATA. Really?

CARIDAD. No.

RENATA. Hmmmmm… I don't know –

CARIDAD. What would you even say to him if you were to call him right now?

RENATA. So you DO have his number?

CARIDAD. Maybe. So what would you tell him?

RENATA. I'd introduce myself and tell him to come over. I just wanna meet the guy, to be honest. Like, I just want to see him in the flesh.

CARIDAD. And the money? The will? What do you think Papi would have said if you had the chance to ask him? Do you think he would've blinked yes or no?

RENATA. I don't know, but I would have convinced him to admit that Eddie is his son and that he has to claim him before he dies. That would've been the right thing to do –

CARIDAD. That's right.

RENATA. At Papi's funeral, it needs to be stated that he is survived by three children –

CARIDAD. What if Eddie doesn't care? What if Eddie isn't interested? What if he's like "fuck that guy, he never cared about me!"

RENATA. That's why I think he should just come over... so that we could, you know...be a family? The kind of family he was never able to have, the kind we all missed out on.

> (**CARIDAD** *refills her glass of wine. She suddenly has this stream of consciousness that takes over her.*)

CARIDAD. Yes, we should be a family. We never know when the rug is going to be pulled out from underneath us –

RENATA. Exactly –

CARIDAD. Because that's it. I'm getting old.

RENATA. We're all getting older, Cari.

CARIDAD. And I'm just this bitter old vieja –

RENATA. No. You are LOVE, Caridad.

CARIDAD. Thank you, Rena...really but I –

RENATA. From the way you cook to the way you dance. The reason why I'm doing good and why your kids are doing good is because we had YOU. Even Eddie. Going from one home to the next... And even though you might feel this hate for Papi, it's only because the line between love and hate is so fucking thin...

CARIDAD. Ain't that the truth.

RENATA. I saw how you would feed him back in the day, I saw how you would look into his eyes, and it was always love and forgiveness...and now you have these beautiful grandchildren who you get to pass down all this generous love to. You're gonna be loved by my baby too, you have to be her Puerto Rican abuelita. And now that me and Sergio and Lydia are grown...we are of service to you.

> (**CARIDAD** *heads to the stove. Magic as she stirs.*)

RENATA. I want you to take a portion of Papi's money and do something for yourself. Go somewhere you've always wanted to go. Do something you've always wanted to do. You got no one standing in your way Cari.

CARIDAD. Sí, gracias. I hear you, nena.

> (**CARIDAD** *kisses her on the forehead.*)

RENATA. Is that sancocho ready yet? I'm starving.

CARIDAD. Sí, casi.[1] We have to wait though.

RENATA. Wait for what?

CARIDAD. Pero puñeta, how many times do I have to say it? It's Sunday and we are having a family dinner.

RENATA. We gotta break the news to them too.

CARIDAD. Sí, claro.

RENATA. You think I can have a snack then? We're hungry.

> (*She rubs her belly and takes out her phone.*)

CARIDAD. *Comer es oponerse a la muerte.*[2]

> (**CARIDAD** *takes out a block of cheese from the fridge and grabs a box of crackers from the cabinet.*)

---

1. Yes, almost.
2. Eating is the opposite of death.

RENATA. I'm texting Carlos right now, telling him to come over.

CARIDAD. Toma. Buen provecho.[3] I got some bread if you wanna make a sandwich.

> (**RENATA** *attacks the cheese. It's her favorite.* **CARIDAD** *sips her wine and watches* **RENATA.** *She dumps the rest of it in the sink.* **RENATA** *sees that.*)

RENATA. (*Mouth full.*) Did you just spill your wine into the sink?

CARIDAD. I had enough for tonight.

RENATA. That's good.

> (**CARIDAD** *holds up a cracker.*)

CARIDAD. The body of Christ.

> (*She eats the cracker.*)

RENATA. Sooooo, where are you thinking of going?

CARIDAD. Galapagos Island. I always wanted to see the baby sea turtles make their journey from the sand to the shore.

RENATA. Yes! I hear it's like witnessing a miracle.

CARIDAD. It is! And right after that I will go to Puerto Rico and purchase a little finca in Cidra. Where me, Mami and Abuela were born.

RENATA. Oh wow. Really? I can help you start looking –

CARIDAD. Lydia already saw it online.

RENATA. Oh! You've already started looking!

CARIDAD. Yeah. Well I always wanted to move to Puerto Rico when I got older.

---

3. Here. Bon appetit.

RENATA. What did Lydia find?

CARIDAD. A little foreclosed home sitting on top of a small
    plot of land, overlooking green hills... Now that Papi
    is leaving this money, I can afford the minimum down
    payment.

RENATA. That's really nice, Cari. I love that.

CARIDAD. ¿Verdad?

RENATA. It sounds beautiful.

CARIDAD. Yeah...that's what I'm gonna do...

RENATA. What about Sergio and Lydia?

CARIDAD. I'll take my grandchildren to Galapagos. You
    leave the Mustang to Sergio. Lydia will inherit my
    farm...

> *(Short beat.)*

And I'm splitting the rest of it with Eddie.

RENATA. You are?

CARIDAD. I've decided that I'm splitting my inheritance
    with our brother.

RENATA. Are you sure?

CARIDAD. Yes. And don't feel inclined to do the same. You
    have a family of your own to think about and you can
    use the money to pay off your debts... I'm the one who
    knows Eddie. I'm the one who owes Eddie.

RENATA. I would do the same if I were in your shoes.

CARIDAD. Gracias.

RENATA. I just...can't believe we have a brother. So much
    time lost. My life could have been so different.

> *(As **CARIDAD** says the following, she brings
> out a third chair and places it at the table,
> she also grabs a book from a nearby shelf,*

One Hundred Years of Solitude, *and places it on the table. She continues to clean and/or stir the sancocho:)*

CARIDAD. I woke up today and I heard the cardinal birds singing in my head. I knew that Papi was gonna die. So I went to the supermarket and bought ingredients for the sancocho. And before you came over I did a limpieza, remember you said you loved the smell of the sage when you first walked in? I lit a white candle for Papi, so that he would be guided by the light. I prayed that Mami would meet him and show him which way to go. I prayed that you would come here hungry and healthy and ready to talk. I prayed and thanked my santos that Eddie walked into Sergio's car wash that day. I prayed that the phone number Eddie gave me that day would still be in service. And I prayed and thanked God when I got a hold of Eddie this morning.

(Suddenly the bell rings... Beeeeeeep. Beep. Beep. Beep.)

RENATA. Eddie?

*(**CARIDAD** nods and heads for the door.)*

*(**RENATA** walks over to the altar. Maybe **RENATA** says the following, or maybe she just feels it:)*

Finally, some healing...

End of Play

www.ingramcontent.com/pod-product-compliance
Lightning Source LLC
Chambersburg PA
CBHW070350120726
47909CB00008B/2789